GANSEVOORT - LANSING
COLLECTION

SPORTING ANECDOTES,

ORIGINAL AND SELECTED;

INCLUDING

NUMEROUS CHARACTERISTIC PORTRAITS

OF

PERSONS IN EVERY WALK OF LIFE,

WHO HAVE ACQUIRED NOTORIETY FROM THEIR ACHIEVEMENTS ON THE TURF, AT THE TABLE, AND IN THE

DIVERSIONS OF THE FIELD,

WITH SKETCHES OF THE

VARIOUS ANIMALS OF THE CHASE:

TO WHICH IS ADDED, AN ACCOUNT OF NOTED

PEDESTRIANS, TROTTING MATCHES, CRICKETERS, &c.

THE WHOLE FORMING A COMPLETE DELINEATION OF THE

SPORTING WORLD.

BY PIERCE EGAN.

VOL. I.

NEW-YORK:
JOHNSTONE & VAN NORDEN, PRINTERS.
1823.

THE NEW YORK
PUBLIC LIBRARY
12915A
ASTOR, LENOX AND
TILDEN FOUNDATIONS
R   1921   L

DEDICATION.

TO THE SPORTING WORLD.

*Better to hunt in fields for health unbought,
Than fee the doctor for a nauseous draught!*

GENTLEMEN,

WHEN the cloth is removed, and the cheerful sparkling glass gaily circulates round the festive board—when the mind is pleasantly at ease—HOSPITALITY the president, and under the banners of FRIENDSHIP, the guests are assembled—it is then the lively *tale*, the *sportive song*, and the interesting *anecdote*, give a peculiar zest to the repast. Each visiter, perhaps, eager to recount the adventures of the day, the FOX HUNTER commences with emphatic raptures, in dwelling on the excellence of his hounds, almost fancying himself still listening to the charms of the view halloo! The SPORTING HERO of the TURF, in his turn, animatedly detailing the fleet properties of his thorough-bred *stud;* the GOOD SHOT, in extacy enumerating the birds he has *bagged;* the admirers of TROTTING, in high glee with the swiftness of their *cattle;* the patient ANGLER, placidly relating the pleasing *nibblings* he has experienced; the CRICKETER, overjoyed at the number of *runs* he has gained; the supporters of PEDESTRIANISM, not only descanting on the exploits performed by their various *heroes,* but of the ultimate advantages the constitution derives from this healthful exercise; the promoters of TRUE COURAGE, too, contending in a national point of view, that the practice of BOXING, through the means of the *prize-ring,* is one of the corner stones towards preventing effeminacy from undermining the good old character of the people of England: and, lastly, though not the least interesting, is the pleasing biographical sketch of some distinguished sportsman, related by the well-informed amateur, with all the characteristic fervour of a theatrical representation; while the company listening to the orator, anxious to catch every trait of the hero in question, yet all harmoniously joining in one general voice,

> To banish *dull care*, or to roar out a *catch*,
> Take part in a *glee*, or in making a *match;*
> Chant the pleasures of *sporting*, the charms of a *race*,
> And ne'er be at fault—at a *mill* or the *chase*.

Under the above lively impressions this volume of Anecdotes has been produced. The most interesting events in all the various diversions of the CHASE, &c. which occupy the mind of the *sportsman*, have also been collected together; in order, not only to *refresh* the memories of those persons who may have witnessed many of the transactions related in this work, but, in fact, rather to prevent any individual from being a silent member in the company of Sporting Characters, by enabling him not to let the *tale* or *song*, stand still, and to take a share in the amusements of the evening, by the relation of any attractive anecdote out of this selection, that may best accord with his talents in recital.

From the extensive and kind patronage the Editor has already received from the Gentlemen composing the Sporting World, he trusts that his collection of select and original "SPORTING

ANECDOTES" will also merit attention, and claim their support.

 With the most grateful remembrance
  of past favours,
   I remain, Gentlemen,
  Your obliged humble Servant,
   PIERCE EGAN.

London, Jan. 1, 1820.

SPORTING ANECDOTES.

CAPTAIN BARCLAY.

This gentleman, in preventing the "Old English Sports" from running into decay, must be considered as the most distinguished *Fancier* in the Sporting World; and who, as a well-known, thorough-bred Sportsman, combining pleasure with utility, founded on practical experience, stands without an equal. Whether he be viewed in partaking of the diversions of the Chase, or paying peculiar attention to improve the system of Agriculture; or in displaying his extraordinary feats of Pedestrianism; or exercising his intuitive judgment in training men to succeed in foot-races and pugilistic combats, Captain Barclay most decidedly takes the *lead*. His knowledge of the capibilities of the human frame is complete, and his researches and practical experiments to ascertain, with a tolerable degree of certainty, the physical powers of man, would have reflected credit on any of our most enlightened and persevering anatomists.

The Sporting pursuits of Captain Barclay are completely *scientific*; and his plans in general are so well matured, that his judgment, nine times out of ten, proves successful.

Robert Barclay Allardice, Esq. of Ury, succeeded his father in the 18th year of his age. He was born in the month of August, 1779; and at eight years of age was sent to England to receive his education. He remained four years at Richmond school, and three years at Brixton Causeway. His academical studies were completed at Cambridge.

Captain Barclay has to boast of a noble and ancient origin, tracing it from the reign of Alexander I. son to Malcom III. King of Scotland, and the 10th of Henry I. son to William the Conqueror, or to the year 1110. And it also appears by his mother's side, that Captain Barclay has an unquestionable right to the title of Earl of Monteith and Air, being the representative of Lady Mary Graham, the eldest daughter of the last Earl of Monteith and Air, who was descended of David, the eldest son of Robert II. by his Queen Euphemia Ross.

The families of the Barclays have not only been conspicuous for their strength of form, but also for their strength of mind. Courage and talents distinguish their whole race.

The Captain's favourite pursuits have ever

been the art of agriculture as the serious business of his life; and the manly sports as his amusement or recreation. The improvement of his extensive estates has occupied much of his attention, and by pursuing the plan adopted by his immediate predecessor, has greatly augmented the value of his property, which is still increasing, and at the present period, (1819,) it is thought, produces ten thousand pounds annually.

His love of athletic exercises may proceed from the strong conformation of his body, and great muscular strength. His usual rate of travelling on foot is six miles an hour, and to walk from twenty to thirty miles before breakfast is a favourite amusement. His style of walking is to bend forward the body, and to throw its weight on the knees. His step is short, and his feet are raised only a few inches from the ground. Any person who will try this plan will find, that his pace will be quickened, at the same time he will walk with more ease to himself, and be better able to endure the fatigue of a long journey, than by walking in a posture perfectly erect, which throws too much of the body on the ancle-joints. He always uses thick-soled shoes, and lambs'-wool stockings, which preserve his feet from injury. In his arms, the Captain possesses uncommon strength. In April, 1806, while in Suffolk with the 23d regiment, although only twenty years of age, he offered a bet of one thousand guineas, which was not accepted, that he would lift from the ground the weight of half a ton. He tried the experiment, however, and having obtained a number of weights, which were fastened together by a rope through the rings, he lifted 21½ hundred weights. He afterwards, with a straight arm, threw a half-hundred weight the distance of five yards; and over his head the same weight a distance of five yards. In the mess room, Captain Keith, the paymaster of the 23d regiment, who weighed eighteen stone, stood upon Captain Barclay's right hand, and being steadied by his left, he thus took him up, and set him on the table. The deltoied muscle of his arm is uncommonly large, and expanded in a manner that indicates very great strength. His predecessors have always been remarkable for their muscular power. Colonel Barclay, the first of Ury, was upwards of six feet in height; and his sword, which still remains, is too heavy to be wielded "in these degenerate days." Many popular stories are told of the feats of strength performed by his great grandfather; and the late Mr. Barclay of Ury, it is well known, was uncommonly powerful. The name of Barclay is of Celtic origin, and implies great strength.

The Captain having completed those measures of improvement which he had so laudibly undertaken, and his estate being brought to a system of management that required little exertion on his part, he entered into the service of his country, and obtained a commission in the 23d regiment. He went to the Continent in the year 1805, his regiment forming part of Lord Cathcart's army, which was sent for the protection of Hanover. He was afterwards promoted to a company, but was not again employed in actual service until the unfortunate expedition to Walcheren, where he acted in the capacity of Aid-de-Camp to Lieutenant-General the Marquis of Huntley. His ardour for the chase was such, that during the seasons of 1810-11, he frequently went from Ury to Turriff, a distance of fifty-one miles, where he arrived to breakfast. He attended the pack to cover, often fifteen miles from the kennel, and followed the hounds through all the windings of the chase for twenty or twenty-five miles further. He returned with the hounds to the kennel, and after taking refreshment, proceeded to Ury, where he generally arrived before eleven at night. He performed these long journeys generally twice a week, and on the average, the distance was from one hundred and thirty to one hundred and fifty miles, which he accomplished in about twenty-one hours. His reluctance to live in a country tavern, and his anxiety to attend his affairs at home, were the motives which induced him to undertake these laborious rides. Although frequently drenched with rain, he seldom shifted his clothes, experiencing no inconvenience from wetness. His connexion with his tenantry is supported by all those ties which naturally bind a proprietor to that useful class of men. They are industrious and thriving. They receive the farms at a fair price; for he knows the value of land, and that his own interest is combined with their prosperity.

Captain Barclay's mode of living is plain and unaffected. His table is always abundantly supplied, and he is fond of society. His hospitality is of that frank and open kind which sets every man at his ease. He is well acquainted with general history, the Greek and Latin classics, and converses fluently on most subjects that are introduced as topics of discussion. He has stood a candidate for his native county, which his father so honourably represented in three parliaments. In private and in public life, Captain Barclay has ever evinced inflexible adherence to those strict principles of honour and integrity which characterize a gentleman.

The following list contains the most prominent public and private pedestrian exploits performed by Captain Barclay.

The Captain, when only fifteen years of age, entered into a match with a gentleman in London, in the month of August, 1796, to walk six miles within an hour, fair toe heel, for 100 guineas, which he accomplished on the Croydon Road.

In 1798, he performed the distance of 70 miles in 14 hours, beating Ferguson, the celebrated walking clerk in the city, by several miles.

In December, 1799, he accomplished 150 miles in two days, having walked from Fenchurch-street to Birmingham, round by Cambridge.

The Captain walked 64 miles in twelve hours, including the time for refreshment; in November, 1800, as a sort of preparatory trial to a match of walking 90 miles in 21½ hours, for a bet of 500 guineas, with Mr. Fletcher, of Ballingshoe. In training, the Captain caught cold, and gave up the bet. But in 1801, he again renewed the above match for 2000 guineas. He accomplished 67 miles in 13 hours, but having drank some brandy, he became instantly sick, and unable to proceed. He consequently gave up the bet, and the umpire retired; but after two hours rest, he was so far recovered, that he had time enough left to have performed his task.

The Captain, in June, 1801, notwithstanding the very oppressive heat of the weather, walked 300 miles in five days, from Ury to Boroughbridge in Yorkshire.

Captain Barclay felt so confident that he could walk 90 miles in 21½ hours, that he again matched himself for 5000 guineas. In his training to perform this feat; he went *one hundred and ten miles* in NINETEEN HOURS, notwithstanding it rained nearly the whole of the time, and he was up to his ancles in mud. This performance may be deemed the greatest on record, being at the rate of upwards of 135 miles in 24 hours.

On the 10th of November, 1891, he started to perform the above match, between York and Hull. The space of ground was a measured mile; and on each side of the road a number of lamps were placed for the purpose of giving light during the darkness of the night. The Captain was dressed in a flannel close shirt, flannel trowsers and night-cap, lambs'-wool stockings, and thick-soled leather shoes. He proceeded till he had gone 70 miles, scarcely varying in regularly performing each round of two miles in $25\tfrac{1}{4}$ minutes, taking refreshment at different periods. The Captain commenced at 12 o'clock at night, and performed the whole distance by 22 minutes 4 seconds past eight o'clock on Tuesday evening, being one hour, seven minutes, and fifty-six seconds within the specified time. He could have continued for several hours longer if necessary.

In August, 1802, Captain Barclay walked from Ury to Dr. Grant's house at Kirkmichael, a distance of 80 miles, where he remained a day and a night, without going to bed, and came back to Ury by dinner on the third day, returning by Cralty-naird, making the journey twenty miles longer. The distance altogether over the rugged mountains was 180 miles.

In June, 1803, he beat Burke, the pugilist, in a race of a mile and a half, with the greatest ease. In the month of July, he walked from Suffolk-street, Charing-cross, to Newmarket, in ten hours, in one of the hottest days in the season. The distance is 64 miles. He was allowed twelve hours.

The Captain now appeared in the Sporting World as a swift runner, and the *knowing ones* were much deceived upon the event. He started in December, in Hyde Park, against Mr. John Ward, to run a quarter of a mile. Two to one against the Captain: however, the latter won it, by ten yards, and ran the 440 yards in fifty-six seconds.

In March, 1804, he undertook, for a wager of 200 guineas, to walk 23 miles in three hours; but, unfortunately, on the day appointed, he was taken ill, and consequently lost the stake.

August 16, 1804, at East Bourne, in Suffolk, he engaged to run two miles in twelve minutes. He performed this undertaking with great ease, within two seconds and a half of the time.

On the 18th of September, at East Bourne, he ran one mile against Captain Marston, of the 48th regiment, for 100 guineas, and won it in five minutes and seven seconds. At the same place, in a race of a mile, he beat John Ireland, of Manchester, a swift runner, on the 12th of October, for 500 guineas. Ireland gave in at three fourths of the mile; but the Captain performed the whole distance in four minutes and fifty seconds.

In 1805, Captain Barclay performed two long walks, at the rate of more than six miles an hour. In March, he went from Birmingham to Wrexham in North Wales, by Shrewsbury, a distance of 72 miles, between breakfast and dinner. And in July following, he walked from Suffolk-street, Charing-cross, to Seaford, in Sussex, a distance of 64 miles, in 10 hours.

In June, 1806, he walked from Charing-cross to Colchester, in Essex, a distance of fifty-five miles, without stopping to breakfast. In the course of the day he rowed from Gravesend to London and back.

In August, he started against Mr. Goalbourne, a great runner, for a quarter of a mile, in Lord's Cricket Ground. Six to four against the Captain: he however won it in fine style, and performed the distance in one minute and twelve seconds.

In December, the Captain did 100 miles in 19 hours, over the worst road in the kingdom. Exclusive of stoppages, the distance was performed in 17 hours and a half, or at the rate of about five miles and three quarters each hour on the average. In this walk he was attended by his servant William Cross, who also performed the distance in the same time.

In May, 1807, Captain Barclay walked 78 miles in 4 hours, over the hilly roads of Aberdeenshire. He remained five hours in the fields walking about, and returned home by nine at night.

In the month following, he made his famous match for 200 guineas, with Abraham Wood, the celebrated Lancashire pedestrian. The parties were to go as great a distance as they could in 24 hours, and the Captain was to be allowed 20 miles at starting, to be decided at Newmarket, on the following 12th of October, *play or pay*. A single measured mile on the left hand side of the turnpike-road leading from Newmarket, towards the ditch, was roped in, and both competitors ran on the same ground. They started precisely at eight o'clock.

The following is an accurate account of the race:—

MR. WOOD.		CAPT. BARCLAY.	
Hours.	Miles.	Hours.	Miles.
1	8	1	6
2	7	2	6
3	7	3	6
4	6½	4	6
5	6	5	6
6	5½	6	6
	40		36

When the pedestrians had performed the above number of hours, Wood resigned the contest; but Captain Barclay walked four miles father to decide some bets. The unexpected termination of this race excited considerable surprise in the Sporting World, as it was known to most people present, that Wood had gone 50 miles in seven hours, whilst training, and on a wet day, and was desirous of continuing his journey, in a state very fresh, but was stopped lest he should injure himself by the unfavourable state of the weather. He had also done, at Brighton, 40 miles in five hours; and he was now expected to do considerable more. Several of those who had betted on Wood, declined paying from the suspicion of something unfair having taken place. It was, however, manifest that Captain Barclay had not the slightest suspicion of any collusion. The regular frequenters of Newmarket said, the bets ought to be paid, although they were of opinion, the race was thrown over, or a man may at any time get off his bets. It was the opinion of Sir Charles Bunbury and other distinguished sportsmen, that men should not bet on a foot-race, but if they did such things they ought to pay. The sporting men from London protested against such doctrine, and declared off. The disputes on this head were finally settled at Tattersall's; when, after some argumentative discourse, it was the opinion of a considerable majority, that the bets ought not to be paid, as it was then well known, that Wood after he had gone 22 miles, had liquid laudanum administered to him by some of his pretended friends, who, to give a show to their designing practices, laid a few bets in his favour of no considerable amount, but procured, by their agents, large bets for considerable sums against him, and that the publican ought to have been indicted with others for a conspiracy.

As an additional instance of the Captain's strength, he performed a most laborious undertaking merely for amusement, in August, 1808. Having gone to Colonel Murray Farquharson's house, of Allanmore in Aberdeenshire, he went out at five in the morning to enjoy the sport of grouse shooting on the mountains, where he travelled at least 30 miles. He returned to dinner to the Colonel's house by five in the afternoon, and in the evening set off for Ury, a distance of 60 miles, which he walked in 11 hours, without stopping once to refresh. He attended to his ordinary business at home, and in the afternoon walked to Laurencekirk, 16 miles, where he danced at a ball during the night, and returned to Ury by seven in the morning. He did not yet retire to bed, but occupied the day by patridge-shooting in the fields. He had thus travelled not less than 130 miles, supposing him to have gone only eight miles in the course of the day's shooting at home, and also danced at Laurencekirk, without sleeping, or having been in a bed for two nights and nearly three days.

In December, without any preparation, and immediately after his breakfast, he matched himself against a runner of the Duke of Gordon's to go from Gordon Castle to Huntley Lodge, a distance of nineteen miles. The Captain performed it in two hours and eight minutes, beating his opponent five miles. Captain Barclay ran the first nine miles in fifty minutes, although the road was very hilly, and extremely bad.

In October, 1808, Captain Barclay made a match with Mr. Webster, a gentleman of great celebrity in the Sporting World; by which Captain Barclay engaged himself to go on foot, a thousand miles in a thousand successive hours, at the rate of a mile in each and every hour, for a bet of one thousand guineas, to be performed at Newmarket Heath, and to start on the following first of June.

In the intermediate time of matching and starting, the Captain was in training by Mr. Smith, the old sportsman, and his son. Previous to the attempt being made, the house of Mr. Buckle, the famous jockey, on Newmarket Heath, was engaged for Mr. Barclay's accomodation. From this house, a course of half a mile was made, and which the Captain was to go and return to the house every hour. On each side of this course, lamps were placed for the convenience of Mr. Barclay in the night.

To enter into a tedious detail of this matchless performance, would be tiresome to our readers: suffice it to say, he started at twelve o'clock at night, on Thursday, the 1st of June, in good health, and high spirits. His dress, from the commencement of his performance, varied with the weather. Sometimes he walked in a flannel jacket, sometimes in a loose dark gray coat, with strong shoes, and two pair of coarse stockings, the outer pair what are called boot-stockings, without feet, to keep his legs dry. He walked in a sort of lounging gait, without any apparent extraordinary exertion, scarcely raising his feet two inches above the ground. During a great part of the time he was performing his feat, the weather was very rainy, but he felt no inconvenience from it; indeed wet weather, instead of being disadvantageous, was favourable to his exertions; as, during dry weather, he found it necessary to have a watercart to go over the ground to keep it cool, and prevent it becoming too hard. Towards the conclusion of the performance, it was said, the Captain suffered much from the spasmodic affection of his legs, so that he could not walk a mile in less than twenty minutes; he, however, eat and drank well, and bets were two to one, and five to two on his finishing his journey in the time prescribed him. About eight days before he finished, the sinews of his right leg, which had been in a bad state, became much better, and he continued to pursue his task in high spirits, and consequently bets were ten to one in his favour, in London, at Tattersall's, and other sporting circles.

On Wednesday, July the 12th, Captain Barclay completed his arduous pedestrian undertaking. He had till four o'clock P. M. to finish his task, but he performed his last mile by a quarter of an hour after three, in perfect ease and great spirit, amidst an immense crowd of spectators. The influx of company had so much increased on Sunday, it was recommended that the ground should be roped in. To this, however, Captain Barclay objected, saying, that he did not like such parade. The crowd, however, became so great on Monday, and he had experienced so great interruption, that he was prevailed upon to allow this precaution to be taken, and next morning the workmen began to rope in the ground. For the last two days he appeared in higher spirits, and performed his last mile with apparently more ease, and in a shorter time, than he had done for some days past.

With the change of weather he had thrown of his loose great coat, which he wore during the rainy period, and performed in a flannel jacket. He also put on shoes remarkably thicker than any which he had used in any previous part of his performance. When asked how he meant to act after he had finished his feat, he said, he should that night take a good sound sleep, but that he must have himself awaked twice or thrice in the night to avoid the danger of a too sudden transition from almost constant exertion to a state of long repose. One hundred guineas to one, and indeed, any odds whatever were offered on Wednesday morning; but so strong was the confidence in his success that no bets could be obtained. The multitude of people who resorted to the scene of action in the course of the concluding days, was unprecedented. Not a bed could be procured on Tuesday night, at Newmarket, Cambridge, or any of the towns and villages in the vicinity, and every horse and vehicle were engaged. Among the nobility and gentry who witnessed, on Wednesday, the conclusion of this extraordinary feat, were the Dukes of Argyle and St. Alban's; Earls Grosvenor, Besborough and Jersey; Lord's Foley and Somerville; Sir John Lade, Sir F. Standish, &c. &c. Captain Barclay had 16,000*l.* depending upon his undertaking. The aggregate of the bets is supposed to amount to 100,000*l.*

Surgeon Sandivor, a professional gentleman of eminence at Newmarket, who had carefully observed him since the commencement of his laborious task, was confident that he could have held out a fortnight longer!!

For a perfect knowledge of the Art of Self Defence, as an amateur, Captain Barclay, at one period, might be said to have no competitor. His *set-tos* with the late Game Chicken, Jem Belcher, and also with the Champion of

England, Shaw, &c. &c. sufficiently proved his great strength, skill, and courage. "Light play" was not one of the traits of the Captain; he spared no one, when in combat, and, brave man like, he never expected any thing by way of "deference to his rank" from his opponent. Upon the whole, Captain Barclay must be viewed as a most extraordinary man; and shows the extent of vigour that the human frame derives from exercise.

THE MOCKING BIRD OF AMERICA.

The plumage of the Mocking-bird, though none of the homeliest, has nothing gaudy or brilliant in it; and had he nothing else to recommend him, would scarcely entitle him to notice; but his figure is well-proportioned, and even handsome. The ease, elegance, and rapidity of his movements—the animation of his eye, and the intelligence he displays in listening, and laying up lessons from almost every species of the feathered creation within his hearing, are really surprising, and mark the peculiarity of his genius. To these qualities we may add that of a voice, full, strong, and musical, and capable of almost every modulation, from the clear mellow tones of the wood thrush to the savage scream of the bald eagle. In the measure and accent, he faithfully follows his originals. In force and sweetness of expression he greatly improves upon them. In his native groves, mounted on the top of a tall bush, or half-grown tree, in the dawn of dewy morning, while the woods are already vocal with a multitude of warblers, his admirable song rises preeminent over every competitor. The ear can listen to his music alone, to which that of the others seems a mere accompaniment. Neither is this strain altogether imitative. His own native notes, which are easily distinguishable by such as are well acquainted with those of our various song birds, are bold and full, and varied seemingly beyond all limits. They consist of short expressions of two, three, or, at the most, five or six syllables, generally interspersed with imitations, and all of them uttered with great emphasis and rapidity, and continued, with undiminished ardour, for half an hour or an hour at a time. His expanded wings and tail glittering with white, and the buoyant gaiety of his action arresting the eye, as his song most irresistibly does the ear, he sweeps round with enthusiastic ecstacy—he mounts and descends as his song swells or dies away; which has thus been beautifully expressed. "He bounds aloft with the celerity of an arrow, as if to recover or recall his very soul, expired in the last elevated strain." While exerting himself, a by-stander, destitute of sight, would suppose that the whole feathered tribe had assembled together on a trial of skill, each striving to produce his utmost effect, so perfect are his imitations. He many times deceives the sportsman, and sends him in search of birds that perhaps are not within miles of him, but whose notes he exactly imitates: even birds themselves are frequently imposed on by this admirable mimic, and are decoyed by the fancied calls of their mate, or dive, with precipitation, into the depth of thickets, at the scream of what they suppose to be the sparrowhawk.

The mocking-bird loses little of the power and energy of his song by confinement. In his domesticated state, when he commences his career of song, it is impossible to stand by uninterested. He whistles for the dog; Cæsar starts up, wags his tail, and runs to meet his master. He squeaks out like a hurt chicken; and the hen hurries about with banging wings and bristled feathers, clucking to protect her injured brood. The barking of the dog, the mewing of the cat, the creaking of a passing wheelbarrow, are followed with great truth and rapidity. He repeats the tune taught him by his master, though of considerable length, fully and faithfully. He runs over the quiverings of the canary, and the clear whistlings of the Virginia nightingale, or red-bird, with such superior execution and effect, that the mortified songsters feel their own inferiority, and become altogether silent, while he seems to triumph in their defeat by redoubling his exertions.

This excessive fondness for variety, however, in the opinion of some, injures his song. His elevated imitations of the brown-thrush are frequently interrupted by the crowing of cocks; and the warblings of the blue-bird, which he exquisitely manages, are mingled with the screamings of swallows, or the cackling of hens: amidst the simple melody of the robin, we are suddenly surprised by the shrill reiterations of the whip-poor-will; while the notes of the kill-deer, blue-jay, martin, and twenty others, succeed with such imposing reality, that we look round for the originals, and discover with astonishment, that the sole performer in this singular concert is the admirable bird now before us. During this exhibition of his powers, he spreads his wings, expands his tail, and throws himself around the cage in all the ecstacy of enthusiasm, seeming not only to sing, but to dance, keeping time to the measure of his music. Both in his native and domesticated state, during the solemn stilness of night, as soon as the moon rises in silent majesty, he begins his delightful solo; and serenades us the livelong night with a full display of his vocal powers, making the whole neighbourhood ring with his inimitable medley.

> Bird of wonder! nature's darling!
> Little vocal prodigy!
> Blackbird, linnet, thrush, or starling,
> All in turn must yield to thee.
>
> Happy mimic! nought can 'scape thee.
> Dog or cat thou can't deceive;

Yet no creature dares to ape thee;
  Man can scarce thy powers believe.

Blithe, surprising, merry creature,
  Fraught with ev'ry other's note;
Pleasing, both in form and feature,
  With a *melange* in thy throat.

Day and night thy worth proclaim thee,
  Sovereign of the feather'd throng!
Well may every songster blame thee,
  Thine exceeds their sweetest song.

All the sun-day thou sit'st singing,
  Flutt'ring on expanded wings;
Peal on peal harmony ringing,
  Sweet as flower of fragrance springs.

By the moon, from night to morning,
  Still thy melody is heard;
Time and place, and season scorning,
  Charming, *matchless*, MOCKING BIRD.

THE MOORISH WRESTLERS;

With some account of their Equestrian Performances.

In Algiers, as well as in other places, on Friday, their Sabbath, in the afternoon, they generally take their recreation; and amongst their several sports and diversions, they have a comical sort of wrestling, which is performed about a quarter of a mile without the gate, called *Bab el wait*, the western gate. There is a plain just by the sea-side, where, when the people are gathered together, they make a ring, all sitting on the ground, excepting the combatants. Anon there comes one boldly in, and strips all to his drawers. Having done this, he turns his back to the ring, and his face towards his clothes on the ground. He then pitches on his right knee; and throws abroad his arms three times, dashing his hands together as often, just above the ground; which having done, he puts the back of his hand to the ground and then kisses his fingers, and puts them to his forehead; then makes two or three good springs into the middle of the ring, and there he stands with his left hand to his left ear, and his right hand to his left elbow; in this posture the *challenger* stands, not looking about, till some one comes into the ring to take him up; and he that comes to take him up, does the very same postures, and then stands by the side of him in the manner aforesaid. Then the tryer of the play comes behind the *pilewans* (for so the wrestlers are termed by them) and covers their naked backs and heads, and makes a short harangue to the spectators.

After this, the *pilewans* face each other, and then both at once slap their hands on their thighs, then clap them together, and then lift them up as high as their shoulders, and cause the palms of their hands to meet, and, with the same, dash their heads one against another three times, so hard that many times the blood runs down. This being done, they walk off from one another, and traverse the ground, eyeing each other like two game cocks. If either of them finds his hands moist, he rubs them on the ground for the better holdfast; and they will make an offer of closing twice or thrice before they do. They will come as often within five or six yards, one of the other, and clap their hands to each other, and then put forward the left leg, bowing their bodies, and leaning with the left elbow on the right knee, for a little while, looking one at the other, just like two boxers. Then they walk a turn again; then at it they go; and as they are naked to the middle, so there is but little holdfast; there is much ado before one has a fair cast on his back; they having none of our Devonshire or Cornish skill. He that throws the other goes round the ring, taking money of any that will give it him, which is but a small matter, it may be a farthing, a halfpenny, or a penny, of a person, which is much. Having gone the round, he goes to the tryer, and delivers him the money so collected, who, in a short time, returns it again to the conqueror, and makes a short speech of thanks. While this is doing, two others come into the ring to wrestle. But at their *byrams*, or feasts, those which are the most famous *pilewans* come in to show their parts before the Dey, eight or ten together. These anoint themselves all over with oil, having on their bodies only a pair of leathern drawers, which are well oiled: they stand in the street near *Bab el wait*, (the gate before mentioned,) without which are all their sports held, spreading out their arms, as if they would oil people's fine clothes, unless they give some money, which many do to carry on the joke. They are the choice of all the stout wrestlers, and wrestle before the Dey, who sits on a carpet spread on the ground, looking on; and when the sport is over, he gives two or three dollars to each. After which, the Dey, with the Bashaw, mount their horses, and several *Spahys* ride one after another, throwing sticks made like lances at each other; and the Dey, rides after one or other of them, who is his favourite, and throws his wooden lance at him; and, if he happens to hit him, the *Spahy* comes off his horse to the Dey, who gives him money. After all which diversions, they ride to the place where the Dey has a tent pitched, and there they spend the afternoon in eating, and drinking coffee, and pleasant talk, but no wine. The Dey usually appears in no great splendour at Algiers; as he often rides into the town from his garden in a morning on his mule, attended only by a slave on another.

The Moors frequently amuse themselves by riding with the utmost apparent violence against a wall, and a stranger would conceive it impossible for them to avoid being dashed to pieces; when, just as the horse's head touches the wall, they stop him with the utmost accuracy. To strangers, on horseback, or on foot, it is also a common species of compliment to ride violently up to them, as if intending to trample them to pieces, and then to stop their horses short, and fire a musket in their faces. Upon these occasions they are very proud in discovering their dexterity in horsemanship, by making the animal rear up, so as almost to throw him on his back, putting him immediately after on the full speed for a few yards, then stopping him instantaneously, and all this is accompanied by loud and hollow cries.

There is another favourite amusement, which displays perhaps superior agility. A number of persons on horseback start at the same moment, accompanied with loud shouts, gallop at full speed to an appointed spot, when they stand up strait in the stirrups, put the reins, which are very long, in their mouths, level their pieces, and fire them off: throw their firelocks immediately over their right shoulders, and stop their horses nearly at the same instant. This also is their manner of engaging in an action.

VORACITY OF THE HERON.

In the month of April, 1818, as a person was walking a short distance from the river Mole, in the neighbourhood of Cobham Park, Surry, where H. C. Combe, Esq. has a *heronry*, he was surprised by a pike in weight full 2lbs. dropping from the air immediately before him; on looking up, he perceived a large heron hovering over him, which had no doubt dropped the fish from its beak. And also during the same month, another individual near the above spot, saw a heron take a fish from the water, and after carrying it to a bank insert its bill into the vent of the fish, beginning to suck its entrails: he drove away the bird, and on taking up the fish, found it to be a pike weighing a pound and upwards.

NABOB AND TIGER.

A Nabob once, for pleasure or for sport,
A tiger kept some distance from his court;
And as in parts where best such things are known,
'Tis wiser deem'd those brutes should live *alone*,
He therefore built, on some adjacent ground,
A mansion strong, and fenc'd with wall around;
Likewise so high, that it was thought, no doubt,
None could leap *in*, nor those within leap *out;*
Yet true it was, (I've heard my author tell,
Who knew the story and the Nabob well;)
One fatal night, as, prowling round for prey,
A ROVING TIGER chanc'd to pass that way;
And by some token, or, as some suppose,
Soon found each other, by mere *dint of nose;*
The midnight hour, with frightful yellings rung,
And on the roof the vagrant hero sprung;
Quick thro' the same his desperate way he tore
With dreadful threat'nings and tremendous roar;
Their active jaws soon foamed with streaming gore,
And bath'd around, with blood, the reeking floor:
Hard was the fight and (horrid to relate,)
The flesh they tore the savage monsters *eat;*
So fierce the war, that, saving teeth and nails,
Nothing was found next morning—*but their tails.*

WEIGHT FOR INCHES.

It may prove a matter of intelligence to those persons unconnected with the movements and terms of the Sporting World, to understand hat the graduated scale for a match, when made for two or more horses to run and carry *weight for inches*, is thus: that horses measuring 14 hands are each to carry nine stone, above or below which height, they are to carry seven pounds more or less, for every inch they are higher or lower than the fourteen hands fixed as the criterion.

Example.—A horse measuring 14 hands one inch and a half, (four inches making one hand) will carry nine stone, ten pounds, eight ounces: a horse measuring 13 hands two inches and a half, will carry only eight stone, three pounds, eight ounces; the former being one inch and a half above the 14 hands, the other one inch and a half below it; the weight is therefore added or diminished by the eighth of every inch, higher or lower, weight in proportion.

These Plates were so exceedingly popular at one time, that very few country courses were without one of this description, and were better known by the name of Give-and-take Plates.

It is therefore seen, that a horse being 16 hands and a half high, will have to carry 13 stone, three pounds, eight ounces; while, in all probability, the knowing sportsman's horse will have to carry 10 stone seven pounds only, making a difference in the weight of two stone, ten pounds, eight ounces. Superiority of speed will therefore be a great point in view before a match is made upon the above condition.

THE LATE DUKE OF HAMILTON.

The late Duke of Hamilton was generally conceived to be a sportsman of the first feather, and his fame on the turf is already so well known, that it would be useless any farther to be his commentator.

Nature had been particularly bountiful to his Grace; his form was manly, his preception quick, and to the strength of Antæus was added the eye of Dicobolus. He had the courage of the lion, and his humanity will be better shown in the following circumstance.

As the Duke was returning to town in his phaeton, his progress was impeded near the King of Bohemia's head, Turnham-green, by a vindictive coachman, who was lacerating a pair of fine young horses, in harness, and using to them language the most indecorous. "Fellow," said the Duke, "if I knew your master, I would presently give him notice of your cruelty." "If you'll get down," replied the savage, "I'll serve you in the like manner." The Duke passed the infuriated fellow, and waited his coming at the Horse and Groom turnpike, where, having arrived, his Grace again reproved him for his conduct; and the other, not knowing with whom he had to cope, once more became still more abusive, when the Duke, giving his coat to his man, bid the coachman defend himself, which he instantly did, and, after a few rounds, was so dreadfully punished as to lie on his back and cry for mercy. "You have it," said the Duke, "though you could show none to your horses, who, though they wanted the tongues to complain, have found a friend in the Duke of Hamilton." The fellow, in consequence of the drubbing, took to his bed, and being turned from his master's service, the Duke allowed his wife one guinea a week till his perfect recovery.

To the great grief of his friends, his Grace was cut off in the very bloom of his youth, and the world was deprived of one whose enlightened conduct ever went to show that man was not born for himself alone—his gates at all times open to the worthy, and his table spread with the hands of liberality.

> If to his share some lighter errors fell,
> This truth let friendship to his mem'ry tell;
> His heart was honest, to the good sincere,
> And scorn'd the pomp of fools, tho' born a peer.
> Nor place, nor pension, ever fill'd his thought,
> He lov'd his country, as a Briton ought.
> Against the wanderer never clos'd his doors,
> But where he merit found, dispens'd his stores.
> Let those, the wealthy, of his high estate,
> Pursue his virtues, and be truly great.

A better cricketer than the Duke of Hamilton seldom stood before a wicket; the best bowlers found much difficulty to derange his stumps, and there was a mark in Lord's Old Ground, called the Duke's stroke; it was of an unusual length, measuring from the wicket to where the ball first fell, 132 yards, a circumstance scarcely paralleled.

For manly exercise his Grace had few equals; he has frequently been known to get him, as he would call it, an appetite to his breakfast, to take a wherry at Westminster Bridge, and to give a waterman a guinea to pull against him to Chelsea Bridge, where, in addition, he would reward his opponent, should he arrive first, which was very seldom the case.

The pugilistic science was a great favourite with the Duke. The following circumstance was related to us by the late George Morland, the painter. The Duke coming to town early with Hooper, the tinman, in his way to Half Moon-street, stopped at the Rummer Tavern, Charing-cross, and entered where Mr. Morland was taking breakfast, who, leaping up at Mr. Hooper's appearance, good-naturedly put himself in a posture of defence. "Ah, are you good at that?" said the Duke, instantly stepping to his phaeton, and returning with the sparring gloves. "Here, Morland," said his Grace, "put them on, and we will have a turn together." In vain did the painter protest his inability to cope with the Duke. Spar he must, and after the Duke had beat him over the chairs and tables till Morland could no longer stand, his noble opponent seized him by the hand, good-naturedly took him in his carriage, and set Morland down at his own house, in the

Edgeware road, Paddington. The Duke was also distinguished for his superior knowledge respecting the breed of dogs.

THE BULL BAIT.

WHAT creature's that, so fierce and bold,
That springs and scorns to lose his hold?
   His teeth, like saw hooks meet!
The bleeding victim roars aloud,
While savage yells convulse the crowd,
   Who shout on shout repeat.

It is the *bull-dog*, matchless, brave,
Like Britons on the swelling wave,
   Amidst the battle's flood.
It is the bull-dog, dauntless hound,
That pins the mourner to the ground,
   His nostrils dropping blood.

The stake-bound captive snorts and groans,
While pain and torture rack his bones,
   Gored both without and in;
One desperate act of strength he tries,
And high in air the bull-dog flies—
   Yet toss'd to fight again.

He falls—and scarcely feels the earth,
Ere innate courage shows its worth,
   His eye-balls flashing fire!
Again he dares his lusty foe—
Again aloft is doom'd to go—
   Falls—struggles—and expires.

SINGULAR PEDESTRIAN FEAT PERFORMED WITH A COACH-WHEEL.

On Monday, the 11th of August, 1817, Blumsell, a painter, in the employ of Mr. Marks, coach-maker, New-road, Mary-le-bone, undertook for a wager of forty guineas, to run a coach-wheel the distance of 30 miles in six hours. The ground fixed for the performance of this arduous undertaking, was the Regent's Park, the circumference of which is about three miles and a quarter; he started at half past one o'clock, and completed the wager at 24 minutes past seven in the evening, being six minutes within the time, with perfect ease. He performed 14 miles the first two hours, and then rested about ten minutes. Great bets were depending, and an immense number of people assembled on the occasion. He was so fresh the last mile as to be induced to challenge a lad, who had been some time running along with him, that he would make the winning post first. He was so completely master of the wheel, that he never let it fall to the ground during the whole distance.

ACCOUNT OF CAVANAGH,
*A celebrated Fives Player.**

"When a person dies,† who does any thing better than any one else in the world, which so many others are trying to do well, it leaves a gap in society. It is not likely that any one will now see the game of Fives played in its perfection for many years to come—for CAVANAGH is dead, and has not left his peer behind him. It may be said that there are things of more

---
* From "*The Examiner*."
† JOHN CAVANAGH died in January, 1819, in Burbage Street, St. Giles's.

importance than striking a ball against a wall—there are things indeed that make more noise and do as little good, such as making war and peace, making speeches and answering them, making verses and blotting them, making money and throwing it away. But the game of Fives is what no one despises who has ever played at it. It is the finest exercise for the body, and the best relaxation for the mind. The Roman poet said, that "Care mounted behind the horseman and stuck to his shirts." But this remark would not have applied to the Fives player. He who takes to playing at Fives is twice young. He feels neither the past nor future "in the instant." Debts, taxes, "domestic treason, foreign levy, nothing can touch him further." He has no other wish, no other thought, from the moment the game begins, but that of striking the ball, of placing it, of making it. This Cavanagh was sure to do. Whenever he touched the ball, there was an end to the chase. His eye was certain, his hand fatal, his presence of mind complete. He could do what he pleased, and he always knew exactly what to do. He saw the whole game, and played it; took instant advantage of his adversary's weakness, and recovered balls, as if by a miracle and sudden thought, that every one gave for lost. He had equal power and skill, quickness and judgment. He could either outwit his antagonist by finesse, or beat him by main strength.

Sometimes when he seemed preparing to send the ball with the full swing of his arm, he would with a slight turn of his wrist drop it within an inch of the line. In general, the ball came from his hand, as if from a racket, in a straight horizontal line; so that it was in vain to attempt to overtake or stop it.

As it was said of a great ortaor, that he never was at a loss for a word, and for the properest word, so Cavanagh always could tell the degree of force necessary to be given to a ball, and the precise direction in which it should be sent. He did his work with the greatest ease; never took more pains than was necessary, and while others were fagging themselves to death, was as cool and collected as if he had just entered the court. His style of play was as remarkable as his power of execution; he had no affectation, no trifling. He did not throw away the game to show off an attitude, or try an experiment. He was a fine, sensible, manly player, who did what he could, but that was more than any one could even affect to do. His blows were not undecided and ineffectual—lumbering like Mr. Wordsworth's epic poetry, nor wavering like Mr. Coleridge's lyric prose, nor short of the mark like Mr. Brougham's speeches, nor wide of it like Mr. Canning's wit, nor foul like the Quarterly, nor let balls like the Edinburgh Review. Cobbet and Junius together would have made a Cavanagh. He was the best uphill player in the world; even when his adversary was fourteen, he would play on the same or better, and as he never flung away the game through carelessness and conceit, he never gave it up through laziness or want of heart. The only peculiarity of his play was, that he never volleyed, but let the balls top; but if they rose an inch from the ground, he never missed having them. There was not only nobody equal, but nobody second to him. It is supposed that he could give any other player half the game, or beat them with his left hand. His service was tremendous. He once played Woodward and Meredith together (two of the best players in England) in the Fives Court, St. Martin's street, and made seven and twenty aces following by services alone—a thing unheard of. He another time played Peru, who was considered a first-rate fives player a match of the best out of five games, and in the three first games, which of course decided the match, Peru got only one ace. Cavanagh was an Irishman by birth, and a house painter by profession. He had once laid aside his working-dress, and walked up, in his smartest clothes, to the Rosemary Branch, to have an afternoon's pleasure. A person accosted him, and asked him if he would have a game. So they agreed to play for half-a-crown a game, and a bottle of cider. The first game began—it was seven, eight, ten, thirteen, fourteen, *all*. Cavanagh won it. The next was the same. They played on, and each game was hardly contested.—"There," said the unconscious fives player, "there was a stroke that Cavanagh could not take: I never played better in my life, and yet I can't win a game. I don't know how it is." However, they played on, Cavanagh winning every game, and the bystanders drinking the cider and laughing all the time. In the twelfth game, when Cavanagh was only four, and the stranger thirteen, a person came in, and said, "What! are you here Cavanagh?" The words were no sooner pronounced than the astonished player let the ball drop from his hand, and saying, "What!' Have I been breaking my heart all this time to beat Cavanagh," refused to make another effort. "And yet, I give you my word," said Cavanagh, telling the story with some triumph, "I played all the while with my clenched fist." He used frequently to play matches at Copenhagen-house for wagers and dinners. The wall against which they play is the same that supports the kitchen-chimney, and when the wall resounded louder than usual, the cooks exclaimed, "Those are the Irishman's balls," and the joints trembled on the spit!

Goldsmith consoled himself that there were places where he too was admired, and Cavanagh was the admiration of all the Fives Courts where he ever played. Mr. Powell, when he played matches in the Court in St. Martin's street, used to fill his gallery at half-a-crown a head, with amateurs and admirers of talent in whatever department it is shown. He could not have shown himself in any ground in England, but he would have been immediately surrounded with inquisitive gazers, trying to find out in what part of his frame his unrivalled skill lay, as politicians wonder to see the balance of Europe suspended in Lord Castlereagh's face, and admire the trophies of the British Navy lurking under Mr. Croker's hanging brow. Now Cavanagh was as good looking a man as the noble Lord, and much better looking than the Right Honourable Secretary. He had a clear, open countenance, and did not look sideways or down like Mr. Murray the bookseller. He was a young fellow of sense, humour and courage. He once had a quarrel with a waterman at Hungerford-stairs, and they say, served him out in great style. In a word, there are hundreds at this day, who cannot mention his name without admiration, as the best fives player that perhaps ever lived, (the greatest excellence of which they have any notion,) and the noisy shout of the ring happily stood him instead of the unheard voice of posterity. The only person who seems to have excelled as much in another way as Cavanagh did in his, was the late John Davies, the racket-player. It was remarked of him that he did not seem to follow the ball, but the ball seemed to follow him. Give him a foot of wall and he was sure to make the ball. The four best racket-players of that day, were Jack Spines, John Harding, Armitage, and Church. Davies could give any one of these two hands a time, that is, half the game, and each of these, at their best, could give the best player, now in London, the same odds. Such are the gradations in all exertions of human skill and art. He once played four capital players together and beat them. He was also a first-rate tennis player, and an excellent fives player. In the Fleet or King's Bench he would have stood against Powell, who was reckoned the best open-ground player of his time. This last-mentioned player is at present the keeper of the Fives Court, and we might recommend to him for a motto over his door—"Who enters here forgets himself, his country and his friends." And the best of it is, that by the calculation of the odds, none of the three are worth remembering!— Cavanagh died from the bursting of a blood vessel, which prevented him from playing for the last two or three years. This, he was often heard to say, he thought hard upon him. He was fast recovering, however, when he was suddenly carried off, to the regret of all who knew him. As Mr. Peel made it a qualification of the present Speaker, Mr. Manners Sutton, that he was an excellent moral character, so Jack Cavanagh was a zealous Catholic, and could not be persuaded to eat meat on a Friday, the day on which he died. We have paid this willing tribute to his memory :—

"Let no rude hand deface it,
And his forlorn—*Hic jacet.*"

THE BUMPKIN AND STABLE-KEEPER.

Young Ned, a sort of clownish beau, one day
Quick to a livery-stable hied away,
  To look among the nags;
A journey in the country he was going,
And wanted to be mounted well and knowing,
  And make among the bumpkins his brags.

The rogue in horses show'd him many a hack,
  And swore that better never could be mounted;
But still young Ned at hiring one was slack,
  And more or less their shape and make he scouted.

A gentlemanly steed I want, to cut a shine,
So that I may be dashing call'd and fine;
And set relations, friends, acquaintance staring—
From London to look *vulgar*, there's no bearing.

True, quoth the jockey, with attentive bow,
And look'd his customer quite through and through;
I see the case indeed, exactly, now,
And have a horse, that to a T will do.
He found the cash was plenty, and all ready,
And mounted to his utmost wishes, NEDDY.

Sarcastically muttering as he rode off,
At thee the natives cannot fail to scoff,
So far, most proper 'tis indeed,
That thou should'st have a handsome steed;
For where *two animals* a travelling hie,
One should be *gentlemanly*, by the bye.

SPORTING CHARACTERS—OR A PEEP AT TATTERSALL'S.

"I wish the Derby was at —." "Why so hasty, my dear Lord?" cried I, stopping Lord

Curricle, as he swung out of Tattersall's yard. "Ha! is it you?" said he; "*you* (with vast emphasis on the word, and in a strain of aigredoux,) are never out of temper. But to be persuaded out of one's opinion—to act against one's judgment, and then to be done out of a large sum of money, is enough, I think, (shrugging up his shoulders, and fixing his eyes on a tall young man near him,) to make any person swear." "I am truly sorry," replied I, "for your Lordship's misfortune. But how did it happen?"

"Oh, d—n sorrow," said he hastily, "Grieving, my dear sir, is folly, and as for pity, I hate the very name of it. There is no such thing as genuine pity; it is contempt that is so miscalled. Just as a fellow passes you by, if you are thrown from your horse in hunting, with 'My good sir, I am really sorry to see you down. Are you hurt? Can I help you?' and off he scampers, a broad grin on his countenance, or his tongue tucked in his cheek; or, as a bolder blackguard dismounts, comes up to you with his pawing and prancing steed hung by the bridle on his arm, bursts out a laughing, but helps you to rise, a rib stove in, or a collar-bone broken, and says, 'My dear sir, pardon my d—d nonsense, nature is so very perverse; I never could, in all my life, help laughing at an accident. But are you really much hurt? my servant shall catch your horse for you; I am truly grieved at your misfortune;'

and off the flies, comes up with some break-neck rider of a friend, with whom he enjoys the joke, and would just laugh in the same way at him in a similar situation, and then tells all the Melton men what a bad rider you are. Is this true sorrow? Is this genuine pity? No, and be d——d to it; it is malice, hatred, and all uncharitableness; it is any thing but sympathy or christian charity; it is, I believe, for I never trouble the Bible, the Pharisee and the Publican—the fellow who thanks his stars that he is not like that poor sinner."

"I did not know that your Lordship knew so much of holy writ," observed I, as I saw him get ease from thus venting his rage, and triumph in his happy quotation, and in his great knowledge of the scripture. He now shook me by the hand, and parted, with "Thank you, my dear fellow, but never, d'ye see, pity me. I have been fooled out of my money, and that's all—Sam, give me my horse;" and off he cantered.

On a moment's reflection, I began to perceive that his Lordship was not altogether so wrong in his strictures of the human heart. How many who seem to pity—who wear grief upon their tongue for our misfortunes, bear a triumph in their heart! How many are there whose pity is a mockery—whose sympathy is an empty sound!

But I now turned my eyes to the tall thin

young man. He was a Dandy—a complete Dandy; and, as every one in high life knows what a Dandy is, I shall not further describe him. He was counting a parcel of bank-notes, and cramming them into a small Morocco pocket-book; the transparency of the notes discovered to me that they were fifties and hundreds, and the bundle seemed rather voluminous. His face was, naturally, the silliest I ever saw, yet it had a dash of low cunning in it; I saw him wink at an elderly Baronet who was standing in the crowd, and keeping up the price of a friend's horses which were for sale; and they exchanged a sly look, which said, "We have properly done the Peer."

As I never was a turfman, and am only a spectator of what our Dandies and Ruffians do, I should never have arrived at the bottom of all this without the explanation which I obtained from Tom Maberly, an old college acquaintance, who was at Tattersall's, selling off his hounds, and whom I perceived in a roar of laughter at Captain Lavender, an Exquisite of the Guards, not long emerged from Eton, dressed as if he came out of a band-box, and storming like a madman, at being *saddled* (as he termed it,) with a lot of horses which he never meant to purchase, but which he was hoaxed into bidding for, and which were knocked down to him at an enormous price. Tom (here was a *pity* again) modestly offered the Exquisite half what he had just paid for the horses; saying, "Upon my soul I am sorry for your being taken in, but it can't be helped, a man must *pay* for experience, and if you will dabble on the turf, and with turfmen, you must be more on your guard."

I saw that Lord Curricle was not so much out in his bad opinion of the world. But let me explain these two transactions. Tom told me that the young Ruffian, (not the bruiser, but a gentleman,) in conjunction with another honest friend, (the Baronet,) had practised what they technically termed a throw-over. The one advised the Peer, motived by superior information, to lay his money in opposition to his own judgment, and the latter was to go halves in the bet. The bet was lost to the tall thin young man, who was, in reality, a confederate with the other; the half, seemingly lost by the Baronet, was returned to him, and the two friends divided the spoil. "Is it possible that gentlemen should practice such vile tricks?" exclaimed I. "Oh, yes," said Tom, "these things are common."

The case of Captain Lavender was as follows: Mr. Squander had, in three winters in London, run through a very fine property; he was overwhelmed with annuitants, book, bill, and bond obligations; and it was very doubtful whether the sale of the estates would cover all his debts—the more particularly as he was to give a preference to his debts of *honour*, namely the money which he owed at play, and some part of which he had been defrauded of by titled and fashionable gamblers, leaving the necessitous workman, the industrious tradesman, and his unpaid servants, to do the best they could. Thus circumstanced, it was agreed that he should migrate to France, and make a rapid sale of his stud, before the storm broke upon his head, and before a seizure of his horses and carriages took place. His friends agreed to attend the sale for him, and Tom Maberly was to give his aid; Mr. Squander prevailed upon young Lavender to keep up the prices of his horses, in which he was assisted by a Buck Parson and the stud groom, who took care not to buy in. The two green horns considered it as understood that the horses were to be bought in at a certain price, and that the money, which they were nominally to give, was to be returned. But when they found that they had actually bought these horses, at prices so much above their value, and that Mr. Squander had already crossed the water, a circumstance which he had not made known to them—they became furious. It was too late, however, their money was paid down, and the amount was secretly sent over to France.

I have no terms of contempt sufficiently strong to reprobate such conduct. If gentlemen can league together for the purpose of dishonesty and of plunder, what can be expected from the lower orders? With such examples, can we wonder at fraudulent bankruptcies, at swindling tricks, or even at open robbery in the inferior ranks of life? Or may we not suspect that honour, which is but the refinement of honesty, as delicacy of sentiment and discriminative equity is but the educated child of probity, has deserted the higher classes, and has quitted the gilded palace to sojourn and to pine in the straw-covered and wretched cabin. Then, indeed, may we say with the poet, that

"Honesty is a ragged virtue."

and that Boileau, so just in all his other conclusions, is mistaken in saying, that "Dans le monde il n'est rien beau que l'equité," &c. But let us turn away from so unpleasant and humiliating a picture to take a general view of the busy scenes at Tattersall's, where Peers and other movers in high life, descend to be quite men of business, at times—where such a large portion of rank and fashion is occasionally assembled—and where I was drawn, neither as a dealer nor for a lounge, but merely to meet a friend, who went to purchase a young ruined rake's fine set of carriage horses, and from whom I wanted to get a couple of franks for the Dowager Lady Mac Tab.

A masquerade could scarcely exhibit more motley groups than the attendants of this place of fashionable resort. There were Peers, Baronets, Members of Parliament, Turf-gentlemen, and Turf-servants, Jockies, Grooms, Horse-dealers, Gamblers, &c. There you might see the oldest and some of the best blood in England, disguised like coachmen, or like the whippers-in of a pack of hounds; there, master and man consulting about the purchase or the sale of a horse; in one place a person of rank taking the advice of a horse jockey or a dealer, on the subject of some match or race; in another, a fat grazier or a flashy butcher aping the gentleman in new boots, &c. and come in order to pick up a bargain; one corner displayed the anxious disappointed countenance of a seller; the opposite one discovered the elate, yet perhaps more completely gulled, buyer, who was paying cent. per cent. for fashion, or half as much again for a pedigreed horse as he was worth, and whose pedigree was, probably, made out only by the horse-dealer. In the centre of the crowd stood idlers, loungers, gentlemen who had nothing to do but to attend sales without purchasing, and to promenade the parks without knowing or being known to any one. These were discernable by the apathy of their unmoved features. A little aside stood some parliamentary characters talking of the last night's debates. Just by the entrance was a band of gaudy ruffians, canvassing the merits of Smolensko; and without stood a knot of Exquisites praising the beauties of Lady Mary. Near the Knight of the Hammer were half-a-dozen dragoons and some life guardsmen, dressed half en bourgeois half à la militaire, with a crooked gambler and a buck clergyman; whilst Lord Wronghead was posted in the middle, with his coachman at his elbow, nudging him occasionally, in order to direct him how to bid for a pair of curricle horses. Some well dressed pick-pockets eagerly on the look-out, and a parcel of led horses and grooms, with some fine dogs, completed this assemblage.

CUFFING ON THE TURF.

At Oxford Races, in 1817, as soon as the gold cup was run for, and the winner declared, an express set off for Brighton to give the office (to use the language of the turf) to certain confederates at that place, where it was previously known that a party of sporting gentlemen, deeply interested in the event, were enjoying the breezes of the sea air. The person going express, being rather above jockey-weight, did not arrive at Brighton until after the party had retired to rest;—early in the morning the confederates received the news of what horse had won, and the nets were spread to catch the gudgeons; several took the bait, but the chief sufferer was a gentleman well known in the vicinity of Drury-lane Theatre, who, on being accosted a few mornings after, on the Steyne, by a friend, with "Well, Sam, how do you do?"

replied, "Oh, I find myself much better, since since I bathed in the warm bath, and was cupped at Oxford."

TIGER AND LION HUNTING IN HINDOSTAN.

The following sporting description of a Tiger and Lion hunt, in the upper regions of Hindostan, in which chase the Marchioness of Hastings took a distinguished part, is thus narrated by this British Lady, (the amiable partner of the Governor-General,) on her return from England to India.

Songhee, 60 miles N. W. of Diblee, 22d March, 1818.

"We had elephants, guns, bails, and all other necessaries prepared, and about seven in the morning we set off. The soil was exactly like that we had gone over last night: our course lay N. W. The jungle was generally composed of Corinda bushes, which was stunty and thin, and looked like ragged thorn bushes; nothing could be more desolate in appearance; it seemed as if we had got to the furthest limit of cultivation, or the haunts of man. At times the greener bushes of jungle, the usual abodes of the beasts of prey during the day-time, and the few huts scattered here and there, which could hardly be called villages, seemed like islands in the desert waste around us. We stopped near two or three of these green tufts, which generally surrounded a lodgment of water, or little ponds, in the midst of the sand.

" The way in which these ferocious animals are traced out is very curious, and, if related in England, would scarcely be credited. A number of unarmed, half-naked villagers, go prying from side to side of the bush, just as a boy in England would look after a strayed sheep, or peep after a bird's nest. Where the jungle was too thick for them to see through, the elephants, putting their trunks down into the bush, forced their way through, tearing up every thing by the roots before them. About four miles from our tents we were all surrounding a bush, which might be some fifty yards in circumference. (*All* includes William Fraser, alone upon his great elephant, Mr. Barton and myself upon another, equally large, Mr. Wilder upon another, and eight other elephants: horsemen at a distance, and footmen peeping into the bushes.) Our different elephants were each endeavouring to force his way through, when a great Elephant, without a *houdah* on his back, called ' Muckna,' a fine and much esteemed kind of elephant, (a male without large teeth,) put up, from near the centre of the bush, a royal tiger. In an instant Fraser called out, 'Now, Lady H——, be calm, be steady, and take a good aim, here he is.' I confess at the moment of thus suddenly coming upon our ferocious victim, my heart beat very high, and, for a second, I wished myself far enough off; but curiosity, and the eagerness of the chase, put fear out of my head in a minute; the tiger made a charge at the Muckna, and then ran back into the jungle. Mr. Wilder then put his elephant in, and drove him out at the opposite side. He charged over the plain away from us, and Wilder fired two balls at him, but knew not whether they took effect. The bush in which he was found was one on the west bank of one of those little half-dry ponds of which I have spoken. Mr. Barton and I conjecturing that, as there was no other thick cover near, he would probably soon return, took our stand in the centre of the open space: in a minute the tiger ran into the bushes on the east side; I saw him quite plain: we immediately put our elephant into the bushes; and poked about till the horsemen who reconnoitring round the outside of the whole jungle, saw him slink under the bushes to the north side: hither we followed him, and from thence traced him by his growling, back to the outer part of the eastern bushes. Here he started out just before the trunk of our elephant, with a tremendous growl or grunt, and made a charge at another elephant, further out on the plain, retreating again immediately under cover. Fraser fired at him, but we supposed without effect; and he called to us for our elephant to pursue him into his cover.

"With some difficulty, we made our way through to the inside of the southern bushes, and as we were looking through the thicket, we perceived beau-tiger slinking away under them. Mr. Barton fired, and hit him a mortal blow about the shoulder or back, for he instantly was checked; and my ball, which followed the same instant, threw him down. We two then discharged our whole artillery, which originally consisted of two double-barrelled guns, loaded with slugs, and a pair of pistols. Most of them took effect, as we could discover by his wincing, for he was not above ten yards from us at any time, and at one moment, when the elephant chose to take fright, and turn his head round, away from the beast, running his haunches almost into the bush, not five. By this time William Fraser had come round, and discharged a few balls at the tiger, which lay looking at us, grinning and growling, his ears thrown back, but unable to stir. A pistol, fired by me, shattered his lower jaw-bone; and immediately, as danger of approaching him was now over, one of the villagers, with a match-lock, went close to him, and applying the muzzle of his piece to the nape of his neck, shot him dead, and put him out of his pain. The people then dragged him out, and we dismounted to look at him pierced through and through; yet one could not contemplate him without satisfaction, as we were told that he had infested the high road, and carried off many passengers. One hears of the roar of a tiger, and fancies it like that of a bull; but, in fact, it is more like the grunt of a hog, though twenty times louder, and certainly one of the most tremendous animal noises one can imagine.

"Our tiger was thrown across an elephant, and we continued our course to the south-west. In a jungle, at the distance of about two miles, we started a wild hog, which ran as hard as it could from us, pursued by a *Soowar*, without success. Soon after, we stated, in a more open part of the plain, a herd of the nilghau. This animal is in appearance something between a horse, a cow, and a deer; delicate in its legs and feet like the latter, of a bluish-gray colour, with a small hump on its shoulders, covered with a mane. Innumerable hares and partridges started up on every side of us. The flat, dreary waste still continued; though here and there, at the distance of some miles, we met with a few ploughed lands, and boys, tending herds of buffaloes.

"In a circuit of about sixteen miles, we beat up many jungles, in the hope of rousing a lion, but without success. One of these jungles in particular, was uncommonly pretty; it had water in the midst of it, in which was a large herd of buffaloes cooling themselves. We returned home at three P. M.; and after a dish of tea, I fell asleep, and did not awake till eleven at night.

"On the 23d, we again set off at nine A. M.

in quest of three lions, which we heard were in a jungle about six miles to the north-east of our tents. The ground we passed over was equally flat with that of yesterday, but it was ploughed. When we came to the edge of the jungle, not unlike the skirts of a coppice in England, and which was principally composed of stumpy peeple-trees, and the willow-like shrub I observed the other evening, Fraser desired us to halt, whilst he went on foot to obtain information. The people from the neighbourhood assembled round us in crowds, and in a few minutes all the trees in the jungle appeared to be crowned with men, placed there by Fraser for observation. After waiting nearly an hour, we were at last sent for. We found him posted just by the side of the great canal, which was cut by the Emperor Firose, across the country, from the Jumna, at Firozebad, to Dehlee, for the purpose of supplying the cultivation of this part of the country with water. Fraser had received intelligence of both a lion and a tiger being in this jungle, which now chokes up this canal. He desired Barton and myself to go down upon our elephant, and watch the bed of the canal; moving slowly towards the south, while he should enter and advance in the contrary direction; the rest of the party were to beat the jungle above where it was very thick, that in most places it would have been impossible for an elephant to attempt to force a passage through it.

"When we had gone about a quarter of a mile down the Nulla, there being but just room at the bottom for our elephant to walk clear of the bushes, we came to a spot where it was a little wider, and where some water had collected.— Here we fell in with Fraser, on his elephant, who had met with no better success than ourselves, though we had all searched every bush as closely as we could with our eyes in passing along. He desired us to wait there a few minutes, while he mounted the bank above to look after the rest of the elephants; though none of us were very sanguine of sport here, from the jungle being so thick, and so extensive on every side. He had hardly gone away, when the people in the trees called out that they saw the wild beast in the bushes on our left hand: and in a few minutes a lioness crossed the narrow neck of the canal, just before us, and clambered up the opposite bank. I immediately fired, but missed her, the men pointed that she had run along the bank to the westward. We turned round, and had the mortification of seeing her again dart across the path, and run into the water, through the Nulla, for some yards; at which moment our elephant became refractory; kept wheeling about, and was so unsteady as to make it impossible for us to fire. However, we followed her up to the thicket, in which she had taken shelter, and put the elephant's head right into it, when we had the satisfaction to hear her growling close to us. Just as were expecting her charge every minute, and had prepared our muskets ready to point at her, round wheeled the elephant again, and became perfectly unmanageable.

"During the scuffle between the elephant and the *Mahout*, we heard the cry, that the lioness was again running down the bank, and a gun went off. She again crossed the Nulla, and saw the patridges start up from a thicket into which she had penetrated. Just as we got our elephant to go well in, she ran back again, and couched under a thicket on our left hand bank, near to which she had originally been started. All this happened in the space of a short minute, Fraser then called to us to come round the bush, as the lioness being in a line between him and us, we hindered him from firing. Just as we got out of his reach he fired; and as soon as our elephant stopped I did the same : both shots took effect, for the poor lioness stirred not from the spot but lay and growled, in rather a more mellow or holllow low tone than that of a tiger. All our guns were loaded with slugs, and, after a few discharges, the poor lioness tried to sally from her covert, and rolled over and over into the bed of the canal below. Her loins were evidently all cut to pieces, and her hind parts trailed after her. This was lucky for us, as her fore parts appeared to be strong and unhurt. She reared herself upon her fore legs, and cast towards us a look that bespoke revenge, complaint, and dignity, which I thought to be quite affecting; perhaps, however, it was the old prejudice in favour of lions that made me fancy this, as well as that there was an infinite degree of spirit and dignity in her attitude; her head, half averted from us, was turned back, as if ready to start at us, if the wounds in her loins had not disabled her. As it was now mercy to fire, and put end to her sufferings, I took a steady aim, and shot her right through her head; she fell dead at once, and it was found, on going up to her, that the ball had completely carried away her lower jaw. Her body was dragged up the bank, and Fraser pronounced her to be not two years old.

"We now learnt, that the shot we had heard, when down below, was occasioned by the lioness having made a spring at a poor man, who stood panic-struck, unable to discharge his piece, or to run away. She had thrown him down, and got him completely under her, and his turban into her mouth. The elephants, all dismayed, had turned back, when Mr. Wilder, seeing the imminent danger of the moment, fired at the lioness, and grazed her side. She immediately left her hold, ran back into the jungle, and across the canal where we first perceived her. This grand sight we lost, by being stationed in the bed below; it was said to be very fine; but then we had, instead of it, several views of this noble animal in full vigour; and with the sight of an hyena, which ran also across the Nulla.

"We then proceeded on the road to Pannuput, on our elephants, five miles to ——— which is a pretty village. Here I got into my palankeen. Wilder returned to Dehlee; and William Fraser and Mr. Barton mounted their horses, and rode on as hard as they could. I changed bearers at Seerhana, twelve miles, and arrived at Pannuput, eleven miles further, at midnight. The gentlemen had arrived about sun-set. After a little bit of dinner, I was glad to go to bed. Next day, the gentlemen told me, they had crossed again Firoz's canal, which appeared very *tigerish*; but that part of it near Pannuput, was the finest corn country they ever saw, and doubly delightful after the fatiguing and dreary wastes we had been in for the last six days. Pannuput plains were, in 1761, (1174 of the Hegira,) the scene of one of the greatest battles ever fought, between the united Musselman powers of India and the Mahrattas, in which the latter were defeated; fifty thousand Mahrattas are said to have been killed; and the battle lasted three days. No traces of the field of battle are left, the whole plain being in the highest state of cultivation. It is a beautiful scene, scattered with fine trees, and the fort (a common brick one) and town highly picturesque.

"William Fraser drove me to Brusut, in his buggy, on the morning of the 24th; and from the plains of Pannuput I first beheld, with an old Highland playfellow, the snowy mountains of Thibet, instead of the much-loved summit of Ben Nevis."

PUGILISM IN ITALY.

It appears in a publication called "*Letters from Italy*," published by Mr. Stuart Rose, son of the late Right Hon. George Rose, that the art of pugilism is among the games of that country.

"Boxing is, I believe, under different forms, common all over Tuscany, but is reduced to least perfection in the capital. There, to recur to poetry for our assistance,

> "Their hands fair knocks or foul in fury reign,
> And in this tempest of by-blows and bruises,
> Not a stray fusty-cuff descends in vain;
> But blood from eyes, and mouth, and nostrils oozes.
> Nor stop they there, but in their frenzy pull at
> Whatever comes to hand, hair, nose, or gullet."
> *Translation of Battuchi.*

"If a man finds himself overmatched at this foul play, he usually shouts "*In soccorso!*" and by the aid of the first comer turns the tables upon his antagonist. He again finds his abettors, and the combat thickens, till the street wears the appearance of the stage at the conclusion of *Tom Thumb.*

"At Sienna, the art puts on a more scientific form. In this city are regular academies for pugilistic exercises; there is a code for the regulation of boxing matches; a certain time for resurrection is accorded to the one knocked down; and, in short, the strife assumes all the distinguished features of a *courteous combat.*

"In this place also, Vicenza, and at Florence, people contend with what may be called *courteous weapons,* that is, with the unarmed fist; but at Pisa and Leghorn, they clench a cylindrical piece of stick, which projects at each end of the doubled fist, and inflicts a cruel wound when they strike obliquely. I am nearly certain that I have seen the representation of some antique statue, with the clenched hand armed in the same manner, and the stick secured to the fist by strings; but I have no recollection where."

TROTTING UPON NEW PRINCIPLES—OR A HINT FOR THE KNOWING ONES AT NEW-MARKET.

It must be admitted that it is not travelling out of our way to observe, that *Trotting* is a sporting subject, and therefore no apology is deemed necessary in selecting the following anecdotes from the " *Itinerant,*"* in which work the *Bolton Trotters* are thus described: "Before I became acquainted with the inhabitants of this populous

---

* Or "Memoirs of an Actor," written by S. W. Ryley, in 6 vols. published by Sherwood, Neely, and Jones. It is a work of considerable merit, and abounds with original anecdotes.

town, I was led to expect a rough reception; that mischief and tricks were the darling study of the inhabitants, and that strangers never failed to meet with insult from what they facetiously term *Trotting*. But I declare I never was in a town where hospitality and good humour were more conspicious than in Bolton. It is true, they are dear lovers of *fun*, but I never was the subject of a *trot* during many years acquaintance, though I believe the circumstance is rather peculiar, as some of our party were *trotted* beyond their patience. The *Swan Inn* being the general rendezvous, not an evening passed without some attempt to raise a laugh, without some *trotting* expedition. A facetious attorney, who wore a cork leg, made in admirable imitation of the real one, and was esteemed an excellent *trotter*, having a dispute with a stranger, about courage, and the different effects pain produced upon individuals, proposed to elucidate this, by trying against his antagonist, which could bear to hold his leg longest in hot water; he who gave in first, to pay glasses round to the company. The stranger, pot-valiant, accepted the challenge; pails were brought in, smoking hot; the lawyer immersed his leg with much seeming pain; the other did the same; and with many awkward gestures, boldly persevered for about half a minute, keeping his eye fixed upon his opponent, who grinned, and distorted his features as if really agonized. At length, unable to bear longer torture, the stranger drew out his par-boiled limb, and declared himself vanquished, at the same time exclaiming, 'That man must be the devil incarnate, or he never could bear it;' and seeing the lawyer in no haste to leave his situation, said, with much feeling, 'For Heaven's sake, sir, desist; you'll certainly lose your leg.' 'And if I do,' replied the attorney, taking it deliberately out of the water, 'I can buy another, they are only three guineas a piece.' The stranger, finding he had been vainly contending with a *cork leg*, was highly exasperated at the deception, and swore 'he would commence an action for assault and battery.' 'You had better call it *scalding and burning*,' replied the other; 'it's a new case, and will afford the counsel some *fun*.'

"*Trotting* is a Lancashire, or rather a Bolton word for quizzing, and signifies the art of being what you are not, or of giving fiction the face of truth; for instance, if a stranger is present, on a fine hot day in the midst of summer, one of them comes in shivering with cold, and pretends he is wet to the skin; the stranger ridicules the idea, and the other lays glasses all round, and leaves it to the decision of the company, who of course give it in favour of the *trotter*. So many stories are related on this subject, that it would be wasting time and paper to repeat them; I shall, therefore, only mention one more, which came under my observation.

It is natural to suppose if a number of thieves were transported to a desert island, finding no one else to rob, they would rob one another: so it is in Bolton; if at a loss for a fresh subject, they *trot* their own party.

"One evening the bar was nearly full, but no subject could be started with effect, till a gentleman observed, 'he did not think any person present could remain silent for half an hour.' One of the oldest trotters, who had often made the room resound with laughter, at the expense of others, fell into the snare himself; and as he sat in the corner smoking his pipe, deliberately laid it down, and replied, 'I'll lay you glasses round, I do not speak for half an hour, provided I am not personally insulted in any way.' The wager being settled, one of the company was appointed to hold the watch, and the silent man looked upon himself as certain of his wager. It appeared that, some years previous, he had been attacked with a slight paralytic affection, that for a short time deprived him of speech; on this the other built for the success of his plan. Pretending to go out for a few minutes, he made the best of his way to the silent man's house, and thus addressed his wife: 'Mrs. ———, I am really afraid to alarm you; but your presence is absolutely necessary at the Swan Bar; your husband, we fear, has an attack of his old complaint, for he has been speechless these ten minutes.' The poor woman, alarmed beyond measure, ran to the inn, took her husband in her arms, and in an agony of grief exclaimed, 'Oh, John, John, what will become of me?' She screamed with such violence, and her agitation was so great, that her husband, fearful of the consequences, jumped up, roaring out, 'Why, thou fool, they are only Trotting!" and thus he lost the wager.

"It is true, this was trifling with the feelings to an unpardonable degree; but give and take was the order on these occasions, so it passed off as a good joke, an excellent TROTTING MATCH! I am glad to say, this practice has been some years on the decline, and is now in a great measure obsolete."

THE UNCERTAINTY OF WINNING.

It has often been the remark of the knowing ones at Newmarket, that all the money that is won upon the heath never goes from it.

> Newmarket is a pleasant place,
> And so are all the *Trainers;*
> For tho' you oft may win a race,
> They keep it as—RETAINERS.

INSCRIPTION INTENDED FOR THE TOMB OF A NOTED GAMBLER.

> HERE lies a LEG! but, what, no other part?
> No! *he was all* LEG—hands, head, and heart:
> His life was past in betting and deceit,
> But DEATH, though oft he tried, he could not cheat.
> And knowing what *this Creditor* was wanting,
> He tried, in vain, his last resource—*levanting.*

>   Whither he's gone his sporting friends can tell,
>   They say "He knew the place, and call'd it *Hell*."

GREAT SAGACITY OF THE ARABIAN HORSE.

M. Rosetti, Austrian Consul General in Egypt, has communicated in the "Mines of the East," some interesting accounts of the races of the Arabian horses, of which there are five: the noblest is the Saklavi, which are distinguished by their long neck and fine eyes. The tribe Rowalla has the most beautiful and the greatest number of horses. Among the colours, an Arabian writer mentions *green*; it appears, however, from the context, that it is the colour which we call sallow. The author affirms that he has himself witnessed, that the animals perceive when they are to be sold, and will not permit the buyer to come near them, till the seller has formally delivered them up, with a little bread and salt.

EXPERT SLINGERS IN PATAGONIA.

The natives of Patagonia carry a missile weapon of a singular kind, tucked into the girdle. It consists of two round stones, covered with leather, each weighing above a pound, which are fastened to the two ends of a string, about eight feet long. This is used as a sling, one stone being kept in the hand, and the other whirled round the head till it is supposed to have acquired sufficient force, and then discharged at the object. They are so expert in the management of this double-headed shot, that they will hit a mark not bigger than a shilling, with both the stones, at the distance of fifteen yards; it is not their custom, however, to strike either the guanico or the ostrich with them, in the chase; but they discharge them, so that the cord comes against the legs of the ostrich, or two of the legs of the guanico, and is twisted round them by the force and swing of the balls, so that the animal being unable to run, becomes an easy prey to the hunter.

UNPRECEDENTED FEAT IN THE SPORTING WORLD.

Mr. Hutchinson, horse-dealer, of Canterbury, on Thursday, May 6, 1819, undertook, for a wager of 600 guineas, to ride from Canterbury to London Bridge in the short space of three successive hours. He started from the Falstaff Inn, St. Dunstan's, at half past three o'clock, and accomplished his task in two hours, twenty-five minutes, and fifty-one seconds, being more than thirty-four minutes within the allotted time, without any accident or inconvenience to himself. After taking refreshment in town, he returned home by the Wellington coach, and arrived in Canterbury at a quarter before three, to dine with the respective parties concerned in the bet at the Rose Inn, where the greatest harmony prevailed; and the company, of which both parties concerned were present, unanimously voted that the Freedom of the City of Canterbury should be purchased, and presented to Mr. Hutchinson, in consideration of the extraordinary feat he had performed with a faithfulness as honourable to himself as it was satisfactory to every individual concerned in the match. At the end of each stage, Mr. Hutchinson dismounted by himself, and was assisted in remounting again; this he calculates occupied rather more than half a minute at each stage. The horse he rode from Brighton Hill to Beacon Hill, run out of the road at Preston Lane; that also, which he rode from Moor-street to Chatham Hill, made a bolt at Rainham, where he had been standing previous to the day: and the horse he rode from Welling to Blackheath, *bolted twice* going down Shooter's Hill, and again upon Blackheath, which occasioned a considerable loss of time. The horses rode on this occasion by Mr. Hutchinson and his companions on the respective stages, were the property of himself and his particular friends, and some of them were selected from the stud of the Wellington coach; all of them performed their journey apparently with as much ease as their rider, who considers that he could have returned to Canterbury the same day in three hours without inconvenience!

The following are the places at which he changed horses, and the time in which each stage was performed viz.

	Miles.	Min.	Sec.
From Canterbury to Brighton Hill	4¼ in	12	45
From Brighton Hill to Beacon Hill	5½ —	14	20
—— to Settingbo rn	5 —	12	40
—— to Moor-street	5 —	12	50
—— to Chatham Hill	4 —	10	30
—— to Day's Hill	4¼ —	12	9
—— to Northfleet	6½ —	17	0
—— to Dartford	5½ —	14	18
—— to Welling	5 —	13	4
—— to the Green Man, Blackheath	5 —	13	7
—— to London Bridge	5 —	13	8

55½ miles.

	Hs.	Min.	Sec.
Total time	2	25	51

A striking likeness of Mr. Hutchinson, mounted on Staring Tom, (a famous hunter, the property of Richard Pembroke, Esq. of Littlebourn Court,) being the horse on which he started, is published, coloured from life, by Mr. Hudson, 84, Cheapside, price 7s. 6d. It is worthy of remark, that Mr. Hutchinson had his watch fastened on the left sleeve of his jacket, in order that he might perceive how to regulate his exertions with ease to himself, and to accomplish his object with certainty. The watch, which was a most excellent one for keeping time, it appears lost 15 minutes during his journey; this loss of time is attributed to the velocity of motion it must have experienced throughout this extraordinary feat.

THE BOA CONSTRICTOR AND THE GOAT.

From M'Leod's Voyage in the Alceste.

The Cæsar, a private ship, was hired at Batavia to bring home the Chinese embassy, and the officers and crew of the Alceste, after their unfortunate wreck in the straits of Gaspar: besides them, it seems, she had two passengers of no ordinary description—the one an Ourang Outang; the other a Boa snake, of the species known by the name of the Constrictor. The former arrived safely in England; the other died of a diseased stomach, between the Cape and St. Helena, having taken but two meals from the time of his embarkation. The first of these meals was witnessed by more than two hundred people; but there was something so horrid in the exhibition, that very few felt any inclination to attend the second. The snake was about 16 feet long, and 18 inches in circumference: he was confined in a large crib, or cage—but we must give the dreadful relation in Mr. M'Leod's own words.

"The sliding door being opened, one of the goats was thrust in, and the door of the cage shut. The poor goat, as if instantly aware of all the horrors of its perilous situation, immediately began to utter the most piercing and distressing cries, butting instinctively, at the same time, with its head, towards the serpent, in self-defence. The snake, which at first appeared scarcely to notice the poor animal, soon began to stir a little, and turning his head in the direction of the goat, it at length fixed a deadly and malignant eye on the trembling victim, whose agony and terror seemed to increase; for, previous to the snake seizing its prey, it shook in every limb, but still continuing its unavailing show of attack, by butting at the serpent, who now became sufficiently animated to prepare for the banquet. The first operation was that of darting out his forked tongue, and at the same time rearing a little his head; then suddenly seizing the goat by the fore leg with his mouth, and throwing him down, he was encircled in an instant in his horrid folds. So quick, indeed, and so instantaneous was the act, that it was impossible for the eye to follow the rapid convolution of his elongated body. It was not a regular screw-like turn that was formed, but resembling rather a knot, one part of the body overlaying the other, as if to add weight to the muscular pressure, the more effectually to crush his object. During this time he continued to grasp with his mouth; though it appeared an unnessary precaution, that part of the animal he had first seized. The poor goat, in the mean time, continued its feeble and half-stifled cries for some minutes, but they soon became more and more faint, and at last it expired. The snake, however, retained it a considerable time in its grasp, after it was apparently motionless. He then began slowly and cautiously to unfold himself, till the goat fell dead from his monstrous embrace, when he began to prepare himself for the feast. Placing his mouth in the front of the dead animal, he commenced by lubricating with his saliva that part of the goat; and then taking his muzzle into his mouth, which had, and indeed always has, the appearance of a raw lacerated wound, he sucked it in, as far as the horns would allow. These protuberances opposed some little difficulty—not so much from their extent, as from their points; however, they also in a very short time disappeared, that is to say, externally; but their progress was still to be traced very distinctly on the outside, threatening every moment to protrude through the skin. The victim had now descended as far as the shoulders; and it was an astonishing sight to observe the extraordinary action of the snake's muscles when stretched to such an unatural extent—an extent which must have utterly destroyed all muscular power in an animal, that was not like itself endowed with very peculiar faculties of expansion and action at the same time. When his head and neck had no other appearance than that of a serpent's skin stuffed almost to bursting, still the working of the muscles was evident; and his power of suction, as it is generally, but erroneously called, unabated: it was, in fact, the effect of a contractile muscular power, assisted by two rows of strong hooked teeth.

With all this he must be so formed as to be able to suspend, for a time, his respiration; for it is impossible to conceive that the process of breathing could be carried on while the mouth and throat were so completely stuffed and expanded by the body of the goat, and the lungs themselves (admitting the trachea to be ever so hard) compressed as they must have been, by its passage downwards.

"The whole operation of completely gorging the goat occupied about two hours and twenty minutes; at the end of which time, the tumefaction was confined to the middle part of the body, or stomach, the superior parts, which had been so much distended, having resumed their natural dimensions. He now coiled himself up again, and lay quietly in his usual torpid state for about three weeks or a month, when his last meal appearing to be completely digested and dissolved, he was presented with another goat, (not alive we hope,) which he devoured with equal facility."

THE PIGEON SHOOTER'S GLEE.

There's no rural sport surpasses
Pigeon shooting, circling glasses,
  Fill the crystal goblet up,
  Fill the crystal goblet up.
No Game Laws can ever thwart us,
Nor *qui tams* nor *Habeas Corpus*,
  For our license Venus grants.
Let's be grateful; here's a bumper;

In her bounty, here's a bumber,
Listed under beauty's banners,
What's to us freehold or manors?
　　Fill the crystal goblet up,
　　Fill the crystal goblet up.
No suspense our tempers trying,
Endless sport our trap supplying,
No ill state 'twixt hope and fear,
At magic word our birds appear,
　　Fill the crystal goblet up.
Alike all seasons in our favour,
O'er vales, and hills, no toil or labour,
No alloy our pleasures yield,
No game-keeper e'er employing,
Skill'd in art of game destroying,
Free from trouble, void of care,
We set at nought the poacher's snare,
　　Fill the crystal goblet up.
No blank days can ever vex us,
No false points can e'er perplex us,
　　Fill the crystal goblet up.
Pigeons swift as wind abounding,
Detonating guns resounding,
See the tow'ring victims fall.
With Apollo science vying,
View the heaps of dead and dying,
Forc'd to pay the debt of nature,
Matters it—or soon or later?
　　Fill the crystal goblet up.

SAGACITY OF A GREYHOUND AND POINTER.

A gentleman in the county of Sterling kept a greyhound and a pointer, and being fond of coursing, the pointer was accustomed to find the hares, and the greyhound to catch them. When the season was over, it was found that the dogs were in the habit of going out by themselves, and killing the hares for their own amusement. To prevent this, a large iron ring was fastened to the pointer's neck, by a leather collar, and hung down, so as to prevent the dog from running or jumping over dykes, &c. The animals, however, continued to stroll out to the fields together; and one day the gentleman, suspecting all was not right, resolved to watch them, and to his surprise, found that the moment they were unobserved, the greyhound took up the iron ring in his mouth, and carrying it, they set off to the hills, and began to search for hares as usual. They were followed, and it was observed that, whenever the pointer scented the hare, the ring was dropped, and the greyhound stood ready to pounce upon poor puss the moment the other drove her from her form, but that he uniformly returned to assist his companion when he had accomplished his object.

A DOG STUNG TO DEATH BY BEES.

In October, 1818, Mr. M'Laurin, brewer, Newtonstewart, removed a very fine watch-dog from his usual kennel to a situation in the garden, with a view of protecting his fruits from the attempts of juvenile depredators. Unfortunately, however, the poor dog was chained very near a bee's scape, the enraged and multitudinous population of which, not relishing the presence of such a neighbour, sallied out *en masse*, and in a mere twinkling, literally transferred the seat of the hive from a cone of straw to the mastiff's body. It was in vain that the generous animal attempted to defend himself from such ferocious and unwonted foes; every time he opened his mouth the bees descended his throat in hundreds, burying their stings in the passage, and, like certain patriots of the biped race, heedlessly sacrificing their own lives to the supposed good of the republic. The dreadful yells of the mastiff at length attracted the notice of the owner and his neighbours; but their assistance came too late, as the poor animal was so dreadfully stung that he died in a few hours.

LEARNED ASS.

Singular circumstance.—A lady, resident in Devonshire, going into one of her parlours, discovered a young ass, who had found its way into the room, and carefully closed the door upon himself. He had evidently not been long in this situation before he had nibbled a part of *Cicero's Orations,* and eaten nearly all the index of a folio edition of *Seneca* in Latin, a large part of a volume of *La Bruyere's maxims in French,* and several pages of *Cecilia.* He had done no other mischief whatever, and not a vestige remained of the leaves that he had devoured. Will it be fair henceforward to dignify a dunce with the name of this literary animal?

GALLANTRY OF AN ELEPHANT.

"A wooden house was, in 1818, constructed at St. Petersburg for the elephants which the Schat of Persia, had presented to the Emperor of Russia. The male elephant is seventeen feet high; his tusks have been sawed off and encircled in golden rings. This is the same elephant on which the sovereign of Persia used to ride with a canopy over his head. Several Persians, who were accustomed to attend on these animals, continue to reside at St. Petersburg. A singular incident took place with respect to the male elephant. A lady whom curiosity often attracted to see him, never paid a visit without taking with her some bread, apples, and brandy. One day the animal as a testimony of his gratitude, seized her with his trunk and placed her on his back. The poor lady, who was not prepared for this act of gallantry, uttered piercing shrieks, and entreated the assistance of those who were standing near. The Persians however prudently advised her not to stir, and she was obliged to wait until the elephant placed her on the ground as carefully as he had raised her."

SPORTING SONG.

Love is just like a *Race Ground*—it is by my soul,
  Where losses or gains may betide us;
We men are the *Racers*, and marriage the goal,
  And Cupid the *Jockey* to ride us,

To start in the race 'gainst a nymph that is old,
  May prove or a gain or an evil;
She's an angel—though ugly—if freighted with gold,
  But if saddled with debts—she's a devil.

The wisest and best, in this dangerous course,
  Have oft been detected in tripping;
For the *curb* of discretion oft fails in its force,
  When the passions are *spurring* and *whipping*.

There remains but one point of resemblance to trace,
  Which the ladies oft find in a lover,
He's eager and warm whilst he strives in the *race*,
  But the *heat*, when he wins it, is over.

SPORTING SKETCHES OF BRITISH GENTLEMEN, IN 1819, WELL KNOWN, AND DENOMINATED THE RUFFIANS——THE EXQUISITES——THE USEFUL MEN.

In the higher circles, a Ruffian is one of the many mushroom productions, which the sun of prosperity brings into life. Stout in general is his appearance; but dame Nature has done little for him, and Fortune has spoilt even that little. To resemble his groom and his coachman is his highest ambition; he is a perfect horseman, a perfect whip, but takes care never to be —a perfect gentleman.—His library consists of the Racing and Newgate Calendars, the last System of Farriery, a table of odds at betting, and the Complete Sportsman. His dressing-room resembles a cobbler's shop, being filled with boots and shoes of all textures, forms, and dimensions. Shooting jackets, racing ditto, box coats, and lots of under waistcoats, with scores of leather breeches, swell his wardrobe and his bills to an immense extent.—His accomplishments are spouting, swearing, milling, driving, and greeking. His companions are dogs, horses, pigeons, and rooks. He takes the ribbands in his hand—mounts his box—miss is by his side—" all right"—drives his mail with four fiery tits—cuts out a Johnny Raw—lolls his tongue out at him—and, if he don't break his neck, gets home safe after his morning drive.— He next takes three hours to dress, looks over his betting book—how much on the Derby? how much on a match against time? when his bill to the Jew is due? what horse to be sent to grass? what to be put into condition? physics his dogs, damns his servants—all right, quite prime; gets drunk; staggers into the conversazione, quizzes the literati, laughs at every body, and every body laughs at him; holds out one finger by way of shaking hands with the lady of the house, finds it a bad concern, brushes in a few minutes, calls in at Long's, takes some imperial punch, floors the watchman, and sleeps in St. James's watch-house or elsewhere, n'importe.

The Exquisite hath perchance retained a little of what was hammered into his cerebrum and cerebellum by his private tutor at the University; he prides himself upon having occupied a place in the Huzzards, even to his amiable Prince's table; he can talk of military manœuvres and of an affair or two in defence of his country; and he is decorated with a mustachio, and may be, with a tuft of hair on his under lip. Though the colour on his cheek is rather equivocal as to its being genuine, and you may wind him at a mile off, yet so prominent a person is he, that you may easily perceive that he was not

"——— born to blush unseen,
And waste his sweetness on the desert air."

In honest English, he is made up, but so well finished that his appearance at the evening party brightens up many an eye.—His composure of countenance, however, is such as to prove that he is too much a man of fashion to love any thing; and his conduct is such as to leave no doubt of his being always ready to sacrifice every one at the shrine of his selfish vanity.—His dressing room and other apartments are filled with a rare collection of pipes and snuff-boxes, for the latter of which, his jeweller will probably soon appear in the Gazette; and his wardrobe is the ne plus ultra of what Weston, Allen, and other expensive tradesmen can afford to give credit for.—His conversation is agreeably unintelligible; he enters the saloon with a self-satisfied air; and if he meet with the husband of a noted beauty, he gives him two fingers, which is a sign well understood in high life, and when held upwards, puts one in mind of a beautiful line in Ovid.

"——Nova cresendo reparabat *cornua* Phœbe."

The Useful Man is almost always in black; his hair very often powdered; or if he condescend to own to a frissieur the appearance of a fine head of glossy well coloured hair, a pair of spectacles spoils the effect, or he is near-sighted, and runs his nose into your face, and is eternally taking up his glass to bring the object nearer to him—Sometimes he takes snuff; and talks prodigiously of the Continent. His learning and his library are not circumscribed; and from his conversation much is picked up which is retailed as original at second hand. He laughs at his patron's jokes; praises my lady's wit; pays attention to the faded beauty, and those to whom nature has dealt out comeliness with a " stinted hand;" corrects the publications of his friends, and is their prototype in all literary matters. He is grave and respectful in his deportment, and decent in every thing. But the superlative excellence which he possesses, and that which constitutes his characteristic utile, is the support which he affords to his patron and dependent, for they are one and the same person—namely, the patron of his success, the dependent on his labours. The useful man, like Proteus, comes to his patron's aid in the most multiform shapes. He is the reviewer of his or her publication; he is the simple and unsuspected narrator of a work which he has somewhere seen—uncommonly novel, very intereresting, very original—a poem or pamphlet fashioned in reality by himself."

ON THE ADVANTAGES RESULTING FROM A SOUND KNOWLEDGE OF TRAINING POSSESSED BY THAT CLASS OF SOCIETY TERMED "THE SPORTING WORLD."

Training is of such obvious utility to the sportsman, that he is well assured, without due preparation, the Race Horse does not possess, in so important a degree, his fleetness ; that Dogs reared for any particular purpose, also require this invigorating aid : and the Pedestrian, who feels anxious to accomplish ten miles within an hour or continue his race for a longer distance, can never attempt such an exploit with any chance of success, without undergoing the process of training. The scientific Pugilist also gains wind and strength by this operation ; and to mankind in general, its rules hold out the blessings of health and longevity. It is thus Captain Barclay speaks of its utility.

The Art of Training for athletic exercises consists in purifying the body and strengthening its powers by certain processes, which thus qualify a person for the acomplishment of laborious exertions. It was known to the ancients, who paid much attention to the means of augmenting corporeal vigour and activity; and, accordingly, among the Greeks and Romans, certain rules of regimen and exercise were prescribed to the candidates for gymnastic celebrity.

The manner of training among the ancients bore some resemblance to that now practised by the moderns. But as their mode of living and general habits were somewhat different from those of the present age, a difference of treatment is now required to produce the same effect.

The great object of training for running, or boxing matches, is to increase the muscular strength, and to improve the free action of the lungs, or wind, of the person subjected to the process; which is done by medicines, regimen, and exercise. That these objects can be accomplished is evident, from the nature of the human system. It is well known, (for it has been demonstrated by experiments,) that every part of the firmest bones is successively absorbed and deposited. "The bones and their ligaments, the muscles and their tendons, all the finer and all the more flexible parts of the body, are as continually renewed, and as properly a secretion, as the saliva that flows from the mouth, or the moisture that bedews the surface. The health of all the parts, and their soundness of structure, depends upon this perpetual absorption and perpetual renovation; and exercise, by promoting at once absorption and secretion, promotes life without hurrying it, renovates all the parts, and preserves them apt and fit for every office."* When the human frame is thus capable of being altered and renovated, it is not surprising that the art of training should be carried to a degree of perfection almost incredible; and that by certain processes, the breath, strength, and courage of man should be so greatly improved as to enable him to perform the most laborious undertakings. That such effects have been produced, is unquestionable, being fully exemplified in the astonishing exploits of our most celebrated pedestrians, which are the infallible results of preparatory discipline.

The skilful trainer attends to the state of the bowels, the lungs, and the skin; and he uses such means as will reduce the fat, and at the same time invigorate the muscular fibres. The patient is purged by drastic medicines; he is sweated by walking under a load of clothes, and by lying between feather-beds. His limbs are roughly rubbed; his diet is beef or mutton; his drink strong ale; and he is gradually inured to exercise, by repeated trials in walking and running. "By extenuating the fat, emptying the cellular substance, hardening the muscular fibre, and improving the breath, a man of the ordinary frame may be made to fight for one hour, with the utmost exertion of strength and

---

* Code of Health, vol. ii. p. 48.

courage,"* or to go over one hundred miles in twenty-four hours.

The most effectual process for training, is that practised by Captain Barclay; and the particular mode which he has adopted, has not only been sanctioned by professional men, but has met with the unqualified approbation of amateurs. The following statement, therefore, contains the most approved rules; and it is presented to the reader, as the result of much experience, founded on the theoretic principles of the art.

The pedestrian, who may be supposed in tolerable condition, enters upon his training with a regular course of physic, which consists of three doses. Glauber's salts are generally preferred; and from one ounce and a half to two ounces are taken each time, with an interval of four days between each dose.† After having gone through the course of physic, he commences regular exercise, which is gradually increased as he proceeds in the training. When the object in view is the accomplishment of a pedes-

* Code of Health, vol. ii. p. 89.

† It is not so generally known as it ought to be, that a salt, introduced into medical practice by Dr. George Pearson, of London, is as excellent a purge as Glauber's salt, and has none of the nauseous taste which renders that purge so disagreeable to many persons. The *phosphate of soda* is very similar to common salt in taste, and may be given in a basin of gruel or broth, in which it will be scarcely preceptible to the palate, and will also agree with the most delicate stomach.

trian match, his regular exercise may be from 24 miles a day. He must rise at five in the morning, run half a mile at the top of his speed up hill, and then walk six miles at a moderate pace, coming in about seven to breakfast, which should consist of beef-steaks or mutton-chops, under-done, with stale bread, and old beer. After breakfast, he must again walk six miles, at a moderate pace; and at twelve lie down in bed without his clothes for half an hour. On getting up, he must walk four miles, and return by four, to dinner, which should also be beef-steaks or mutton-chops, with bread and beer, as at breakfast. Immediately after dinner, he must resume his exercise by running half a mile at the top of his speed, and walking six miles at a moderate pace. He takes no more exercise for that day, but retires to bed about eight, and next morning proceeds in the same manner. After having gone on in this regular course for three or four weeks, the pedestrian must take a four mile sweat, which is produced by running four miles in flannel, at the top of his speed. Immediately on returning, a hot liquor is prescribed, in order to promote the perspiration, of which he must drink one English pint. It is termed sweating liquor, and is composed of the following ingredients, viz:—one ounce of caraway seed, half an ounce of coriander seed, one ounce of root liquorice, and half an ounce of sugar candy, mixed with two bottles of cider, and boiled down to one half. He is then put to bed in his flannels, and being covered with six or eight pair of blankets, and a feather bed, must remain in this state from twenty-five to thirty minutes; when he is to be taken out and rubbed perfectly dry. Being then well wrapped up in a great coat, he walks out gently for two miles to breakfast, which, on such occasions, should consist of a roasted fowl. He afterwards proceeds with his usual exercise. These sweats are continued weekly, till within a few days of the performance of the match, or, in other words, he must undergo three or four of these operations. If the stomach of the pedestrian be foul, an emetic or two must be given about a week before the conclusion of the training, and he is now supposed to be in the highest condition. Besides his usual or regular exercise, a person under training ought to employ himself in the intervals in every kind of exertion which tends to activity, such as crickets, bowls, throwing quoits, &c. that during the whole day, both body and mind may be constantly occupied.

The diet, or regimen, is the next point of consideration, and it is very simple. As the intention of the trainer is to preserve the strength of the pedestrian, he must take care to keep him in good condition by nourishing food. Animal diet is alone prescribed, and beef and mutton are preferred. The lean of fat beef, cooked in steaks, with very little salt, is the best, and it should be rather under-done than otherwise. Mutton being reckoned easy of digestion, may be occasionally given, to vary the diet, and gratify the taste. The legs of fowls are highly esteemed. It is preferable to have the meat BROILED, as much of its nutritive quality is lost by *roasting or boiling*.* Biscuit and stale bread are the only preparation of vegetable matter which are permitted to be given; and every thing inducing *flatulency* must be carefully avoided. Veal and lamb are never allowed, nor pork, which operates as a laxative on some people; and all fat or greasy substances are prohibited, as they induce bile, and consequently injure the stomach. But it has been proved by experience, that the lean meat contains more nourishment than the fat, and in every case the most substantial food is preferable to any other kind.

Vegetables, such as turnips, carrots, or potatoes, are never given, as they are watery, and of difficult digestion. On the same principle fish must be avoided, and, besides, they are not sufficiently nutricious. Neither butter nor

---

* "It may serve as a preliminary rule, that fresh meat is the most wholesome and nourishing. To preserve these qualities, however, it ought to be dressed so as to remain tender and juicy; for it is by this means it will be easily digested, and afford most nourishment."—*Willich on Diet and Regimen*, p. 313.

cheese is allowed; the one being very indigestible, and the other apt to turn rancid on the stomach. Eggs are also fo bidden, excepting the yolk, taken raw in the morning. And it must be remarked, that salt, spices, and all kinds of seasonings, with the exception of vinegar, are prohibited.

With respect to liquors, they must always be taken cold; and home-brewed beer, old, but not bottled, is the best. A little red wine, however, may be given to those who are fond of malt liquor, but never more than half a pint after dinner. Too much liquor swells the abdomen, and of course injures the breath. The quantity of beer, therefore, should not exceed three pints during the whole day, and it must be taken with breakfast and dinner, no supper being allowed. Water is never given alone, and ardent spirits are strictly prohibit d, however diluted. It is an established rule to avoid liquids as much as possible, and no more liquor of any kind is allowed to be taken than what is merely requisite to quench the thirst. Milk is never allowed, as it curdles on the stomach. Soups are not used;* nor is any thing liquid taken warm but gruel or broth, to promote the operation of physic; and the sweating liquor

* " Broths and soups require little digestion, weaken the stomach, and are attended by all the pernicious effects of other warm and relaxing drink.—*Willich on Diet*, &c. p. 304.

mentioned above. The broth must be cooled, in order to take off the fat, when it may be again warmed; or beef-tea may be used in the same manner, with little or no salt. In the days between the purges, the pedestrian must be fed as usual, strictly adhering to the nourishing diet, by which he is invigorated.

Profuse sweating is resorted to as an expedient for removing the superfluities of flesh and fat. Three or four sweats are generally requisite, and they may be considered the severest of part of the process.

Emetics are only prescribed if the stomach be disordered, which may sometimes happen, when due care is not taken to proportion the quantity of food to the digestive powers; but, in general, the quantity of aliment is not limited by the trainer, but left entirely to the discretion of the pedestrian, whose appetite would regulate him in this respect. Although the chief parts of the training system depend upon sweating exercise and feeding, yet the object to be obtained by the pedestrian would be defeated, if they were not adjusted each to the other, and to his constitution. The skilful trainer will, therefore, constantly study the progress of his art, by observing the effects of the process separately, and in combination.

If a man retain his health and spirits during the process, improve in wind, and increase in strength, it is certain that the object intended will be obtained. But, if otherwise, it is to be apprehended that some defect exists, through the unskilfulness or mismanagement of the trainer, which ought instantly to be remedied by such alterations as the circumstances of the case may demand. It it evident, therefore, that, in many instances, the trainer must be guided by his judgment, and that no fixed rules of management can, with absolute certainty be depended upon, for producing an invariable and determinate result.

It is further necessary to remark, that the trainer, before he proceeds to apply his theory, should make himself acquainted with the constitution and habits of his patient, that he may be able to judge how far he can, with safety, carry the different parts of the process. The nature of his disposition should also be known, that every cause of irritation may be avoided; for, as it requires great patience and perseverance to undergo training, every expedient to sooth and encourage the mind should be adopted.

It is impossible to fix a precise period for the completion of the training process, as it depends upon the condition of the pedestrian; but from two to three months, in most cases, will be sufficient, especially if he be in tolerable condition at the commencement, and possessed of sufficient perseverance and courage to submit cheerfully to the privations and hardships to which he must unavoidably be subjected.

Training is indispensibly necessary to those who are to engage in corporeal exertions beyond their ordinary powers. Pedestrians, therefore, who are matched either against others or against time, and pugilists who engage to fight, must undergo the training process before they contend, as the issue of the contest, if their powers be nearly equal, will, in a great measure, depend upon their relative condition. But the advantages of the training system are not confined to pedestrians and pugilists alone, they extend to every man; and were training generally introduced, instead of medicines, as an expedient for the prevention and cure of diseases, its beneficial consequences would promote his happiness and prolong his life.

It is well known to physiologists that both the solids and fluids which compose the human frame are successively absorbed and deposited; hence a perpetual renovation of the part ensues, regulated, as they are, by the nature of our food and general habits.* It, therefore, follows, that our health, vigour, and activity must depend upon our regimen and exercise; or, in other words, upon the observance of those rules which constitute the theory of the training process. The effect has accordingly corresponded with the cause in all instances where training has been adopted; and although not commonly resorted to as the means of restoring invalids to

* Bell's Anatomy, vol. i. p. 12.

health, yet there is every reason to believe that it would prove effectual in curing many obstinate diseases, such as the gout, rheumatism, bilious complaints, &c.

"Training (says Mr. Jackson) always appears to improve the state of the lungs; one of the most striking effects is to improve the wind, that is, it enables a man to draw a larger inspiration, and to hold his breath longer." He further observes, by training the mental faculties are also improved. The attention is more ready, and the perception more acute, probably owing to the clearness of the stomach and better digestion.*

It has been made a question whether training produces a lasting or only temporary effect on the constitution. It is undeniable, that if a man be brought to a better condition, if corpulency and the impurities of his body disappear, and if his wind and strength be improved by any process whatever, his good state of health will continue, until some derangement of his frame shall take place from accidental or natural causes. If he shall relapse into intemperance, or neglect the means of preserving his health, either by omitting to take the necessary exercise, or by indulging in debilitating propensities, he must expect such encroachments to be made on his constitution as must soon unhinge his system.

* Code of Health, vol. ii. p. 108.

But if he shall observe a different plan, the beneficial effects of the training process will remain until the gradual decay of his natural functions shall, in mature old age, intimate the approach of his dissolution.

The ancients entertained this opinion:— "They were," says Dr. Buchan, "by no means unacquainted with or inattentive to these instruments of medicine, although modern practitioners appear to have no idea of removing disease or restoring health, but by pouring drugs into the stomach. Herodicus is said to have been the first who applied the exercises and regimen of the gymnasium to the removal of disease or the maintenance of health.—Among the Romans, Asclepiades carried this so far that he is said by Celsus almost to have banished the use of internal remedies from his practice. He was the inventor of pensile beds, which were used to induce sleep, and of various other modes of exercise and gestation, and rose to great eminence, as a physician in Rome. In his own person he afforded an excellent example of the wisdom of his rules and the propriety of his regimen. Pliny tells us that, in early life, he made a public profession that he would agree to forfeit all pretensions to the name of a Physician, should he ever suffer from sickness or die but of old age; and what is more extraordinary, he fulfilled his promise, for he lived upwards of a century, and at last was killed by a fall down stairs."*

It may, therefore, be admitted that the beneficial consequences, both to the body and mind, arising from training, are not merely temporary, but may be made permanent by proper care and attention. The simplicity of the rules is a great recommendation to those who may be desirous of trying the experiment, and the whole process may be resolved into the following principles:—1st. The evacuating, which cleanses the stomach and intestines. 2. The sweating, which takes off the superfluities of flesh and fat. 3. The daily course of exercise, which improves the wind and strengthens the muscles. Lastly, the regimen, which nourishes and invigorates the body.

The criterion by which it may be known whether a man be in a good condition, or, what is the same thing, has been properly trained, is the state of the skin, which becomes smooth, elastic, and well coloured, or transparent! The flesh is also firm and the person trained feels himself light and full of spirits. But in the progress of the Training, his condition may be ascertained by the effect of the sweats, which cease to reduce his weight, and by the manner in which he performs one mile at the top of his speed, as to walk a hundred, and therefore, if he performs

---

* Code of Health. vol. ii. p. 123.

this short distance well, it may be concluded that his condition is perfect, or that he has derived all the advantages which can possibly result from the training process.

The manner of Training jockeys is different from that which is applicable to pedestrians and pugilists. In regard to jockeys, it is generally wasting, with the view to reduce their weight. This is produced by purgatives, emetics, sweats, and starvation. Their bodily strength is of no importance, as they have only to manage the reins of the courser, whose fleetness depends upon the weight he carries ; and the muscular power of the rider is of no consequence to the race, provided it be equal to the fatigue of a three or four mile heat.

Training for Pugilism is nearly the same as for Pedestrianism, the object in both being principally to obtain additional wind and strength. But it will be best illustrated by a detail of the process observed by Crib, the Champion of England, preparatory to his grand battle with Molineaux, which took place on the 29th of September, 1811.

"The Champion arrived at Ury on the 7th of July of that year. He weighed sixteen stone : and from his mode of living in London, and the confinement of a crowded city, he had become corpulent, big-bellied, full of gross humours, and short-breathed : and it was with difficulty he could walk ten miles. He first went through a course of physic, which consisted of three doses; but for two weeks he walked about as he pleased, and generally traversed the woods and plantations with a fowling-piece in his hand. The reports of his musket resounded every where through the groves and the hollows of that delightful place, to the great terror of the magpies and wood-pigeons.

"After amusing himself in this way for about a fortnight, he then commenced his regular walking exercise, which at first was about ten or twelve miles a day. It was soon after increased to eighteen or twenty; and he ran regularly, morning and evening a quarter of a mile at the top of his speed. In consequence of his physic and exercise, his weight was reduced, in the course of five weeks, from sixteen stone to fourteen and nine pounds. At this period, he commenced his sweats, and took three during the month he remained at Ury afterwards; and his weight was gradually reduced to thirteen stone and five pounds, which was ascertained to be his pitch of condition, as he would not reduce further without weakening.

"During the course of his training the Champion went twice to the Highlands, and took strong exercise. He walked to Mar Lodge, which is about sixty miles distant from Ury, where he arrived to dinner on the second day, being now able to go thirty miles a day with ease, and probably he could have walked twice as far if it had been necessary. He remained in the Highlands about a week each time, and amused himself with shooting. The principal advantage which he derived from these expeditions was the severe exercise he was obliged to undergo in following Capt. Barclay. He improved more in strength and wind by his journeys to the Highlands than by any other part of the training process.

"His diet and drink were the same as used in the pedestrian regimen, and in other respects, the rules previously laid down were generally applied to him. That he was brought to his ultimate pitch of condition, was evident from the high state of health and strength in which he appeared when he mounted the stage to contend with Molineaux, who has since confessed, that when he saw his fine condition he totally despaired of gaining the battle.

"Crib was altogether about eleven weeks under training, but he remained only nine weeks at Ury. Besides his regular exercise, he was occasionally employed in sparring at Stonehaven, where he gave lessons in the pugilistic art. He was not allowed much rest, but was constantly occupied in some active employment. He enjoyed good spirits, being at the time fully convinced that he would beat his antagonist. He was managed, however, with great address, and the result corresponded with the wishes of his friends.

"It would be perhaps improper, while speaking of Crib, to omit mentioning, that, during his residence in the north of Scotland, he conducted himself in all respects with much propriety. He showed traits of a feeling, humane, and charitable disposition on various occasions— While walking along Union-street, in Aberdeen, he was accosted by a woman apparently in great distress. Her story affected him, and the emotions of his heart became evident in the muscles of his face. He gave her all the silver he had in his pocket—' God bless your Honour.' she said; ' ye surely are not an ordinary man !'—This circumstance is mentioned with the more pleasure, as it affords one instance at least, in the mistaken opinion, that professional pugilists are ferocious, and totally destitute of the better propensities of mankind. The illustrious Mr. Wyndham entertained juster sentiments of the pugilistic art, as evinced by a print he presented to Mr. Jackson, as a mark of his esteem. In one compartment, an Italian darting his stiletto at his victim is represented; and in the other, the combat of two Englishmen in a ring. For this celebrated genius was always of opinion that nothing tended more to preserve among the English peasantry those sentiments of good faith and honour which have ever distinguished them from the natives of Italy and Spain, than the frequent practice of fair and open Boxing."

EPISTLE FROM TOM CRIB TO BIG BEN,

Concerning some foul play in a late transaction.

What! Ben, my big hero, is this thy renown?
Is this the new go?—kick a man when he's down!
When the foe is kock'd under, to tread on him then—
By the fist of my father, I blush for thee, Ben.
"Foul! foul!" all the lads of the fancy exclaim—
Charley Shock is electrified—Belcher spits flame—
And Molineax—ay, even Blackey cries " Shame!"
Time was when John Bull little difference spied
'Twixt the foe at his feet and the friend at his side;
When he found (such his humour in fighting and eating)
His foe, like his beef-steak, the sweeter for beating.
But this comes, master Ben, of your curs't foreign notions,
Your trinkets, wigs, thingumbobs, gold lace and lotions;
Your Noyeaus, Caracoas, and the devil knows what—
(One swig of *Blue Ruin** is worth a whole lot.)
Your great and small *crosses!* my eyes, what a brood!
(A cross-buttock from me would do some of them good;)
Which have spoilt you, till hardly a drop, my old porpoise,
Of pure English claret is left in your *corpus;*
And (as Jim says) the only one trick, good or bad,
Of the fancy you're up to, is *fibbing*, my lad!
Hence it comes—BOXIANA,† disgrace to thy page!—
Having floor'd by good luck, the first *swell* of the age,
Having conquered the *prime one* that *mill'd* us all round,
You kick'd him, old Ben, as he gasp'd on the ground;
Ay—just at the time to show spunk, if you'd got any—
Kick'd him, and jaw'd him, and *lagg'd*‡ him to Botany.
Oh, shade of the Cheesemonger! § you, who, alas!
Doubled up, by the dozen, those Mounseers in brass,

---

* Gin.

† Lives of all the Boxers, published by Sherwood & Co. 2 vols. 1*l.* 6*s.* embellished with 36 portraits.

‡ Transported.

§ A Life-guardsman, one of the Fancy, who distinguished himself, and was killed, in a late memorable set-to,

On that great day of milling, when blood lay in lakes,
When kings held the bottle and Europe the stakes—
Look down upon Ben—see him, dunghill all o'er,
Insult the fall'n foe, that can harm him no more!
Out cowardly *spooney!*—again and again,
By the fist of my father, I blush for thee, Ben.
To show the *white feather** is many men's doom,
But what of one feather, Ben shows a whole PLUME!

THE OWLERY AT ARUNDLE CASTLE.

This "curious fancy" of the late Duke of Norfolk is thus described by the Rev. John Evans. "We were unwilling to leave this venerable castle without the sight of the owls, which are said to be the finest in Great Britain. We were introduced to an utterly ruined part of the ancient castle, where, upon entering the enclosure, we saw a number of these strange looking creatures, hopping about, with an ungraceful gait, and staring at us with looks of wonderful sagacity. One stood at the mouth of a subterraneous excavation, and upon the keeper pronouncing bow wow, the owl instantly returned the expression, retiring at the same time gradually back again into its hole, till it had actually got out of sight. The other owls were driven by the keeper into one corner of the yard; they ranged themselves along a piece of old timber, altogether, presenting a spectacle which raised in my mind some singular emotions. The countenance of the largest of them was marked by an unusual degree of solemnity.

* Exhibit symptoms of terror.

' An owl of grave deport and mein,
Who like the Turk, was seldom seen,
Within a ruin chose his station,
As fit for prey or contemplation :
Upon a beam, see how he sits,
And nods and seems to think by fits.
So have I seen a man of news,
Or post-boy, or Gazette peruse ;
Smoke nod, and talk with voice profound,
And fix the fate of Europe round.'

"These owls are the finest of the horned kind, and the keeper shared no small pride in the exhibition of them. Beauty, Beauty, was the name by which he called them together, and they seemed to recognise the propriety of the appellation with a becoming consciousness. Upon the justness of this term, however, the keeper and myself were by no mean's agreed.

"With respect to the sight of the owls, they are so overpowered by the brightness of the day, that they are obliged to remain in the same spot without stirring ; and when they are forced to leave their retreat, their flight is tardy and interrupted, being afraid of striking against the intervening obstacles. The other birds, perceiving their constrained situation, delight to insult—the tit-mouse, the finch, the red-breast, the jay, the thrush, &c. assemble to enjoy the sport. The bird of night remains perched upon a branch, motionless and confounded ; hears their cries, which are incessantly repeated, but it answers them only with insignificant gestures, turning round its head and its body with a foolish air. It even suffers itself to be assaulted without making resistance; the smallest, the weakest of its enemies, are the most eager to torment and to turn into ridicule. The keep in which the owls are shown is an undoubted remnant of the original Saxon building, and well worth the attention of the antiquary."

This owlery is thus spoken of by another visiter: "The owls, which are still to be seen, are uncommonly elegant birds, and extremely large, some of them measuring across the wings, when extended, from eight to ten feet. Their plumage is particularly beautiful, and their eyes brilliant. The late Duke procured them from North America."

BEAR-BAITING IN OLDEN TIMES.

Bear-baiting was a favourite amusement of our ancestors. Sir Thomas Pope entertained Queen Mary and the Princess Elizabeth, at Hatfield, with a grand exhibition of "Bear-baiting, with which their highnesses were right well content." Bear-baiting was part of the amusement of Elizabeth, among "the princely pleasures of Kenilworth Castle." Rowland White, speaking of the Queen, then in her 67th year, says—"Her Majesty is very well. This day she appoints a Frenchman to do feats upon a rope in the Conduit Court. To-morrow she has commanded the bears, the bull, and the ape, to be bayted in the tilt yard. Upon Wednesday she will have solemne dawnchig."

The office of Chief Master of the Bears, was held under the crown with a salary of 16d. per diem. Whenever the King chose to entertain himself or his visiters with this sport, it was the duty of the Master to provide bears and dogs, and to superintend the baiting; and he was invested with unlimited authority to issue commissions, and to send his officers into every county in England, who were empowered to seize and take away any bears, bulls, or dogs, that they thought meet for his Majesty's service.

The latest record by which this diversion was publicly authorized, is a grant to Sir Saunders Duncome, Oct. 11, 1561, for the sole practice and profit of the fighting and combating of wild and domestic beasts within the realm of England for the space of fourteen years.

Occasional exhibitions of this kind were continued till about the middle of the 18th century.

PORTRAIT OF A JOCKEY.
From Grainger's Characters.

"To ride this season—An able jockey, fit to start for Match or sweep stakes, or King's Plate, well sized, can mount 12 stone or strip to a feather, sound wind and limb, and free from blemishes. He was got by Yorkshire Tom, out of full sister of Deptford Nan; his grandam was the German princess, and his great grandam was daughter by Moll Flanders. His sire won the King's plate at York and Hambleton, the Ladies' subscription purse at Nottingham, the give and take at Lincoln, and the sweep-stakes at Newmarket. His grandsire beat Sam Chifney at Epsom and Byrford, and Patrick M'Chatham over the Curragh of Kildare. His great great grandam rode for King Charles II. and so noble is the blood that flows in this jockey's veins, that none of his family was ever distanced, stood five feet five, or weighed more than twelve stone."

FEMALE PEDESTRIANISM.

On Wednesday, October 29, 1817, Esther Crosier undertook the fatiguing task of walking one thousand miles in 20 days, at the Washway, Brixton, but in consequence of some dispute, she gave it up, after having completed three hundred and fifty miles in seven days.

ATHLETIC SPORTS IN AMERICA.

From the Travels of Mr. John Palmer, *in 1817, through the United States of America, and Lower Canada.*

"Off from Hagerstown, before break of day. The same magnificent scenery, and the same bad roads. It is astonishing how good the stage horses are in this ragged country—you seldom see any blind, sprained or lame: our driver informs us they are very hardy, and with gentle driving never tire. A team of four prime, and matches, is worth six hundred dollars, and will fetch seven hundred dollars in Philadelphia and Baltimore. Small flies do not trouble the horses here as in England, never pursuing them in a swarm round the horse's head. There is a small brown swamp horse fly, and two sorts of hornets, black and yellow, rather numerous, and occasionally troublesome. Women all travel on horseback in these mountainous regions—it would be next to impossible for them to travel any other way till the turnpike roads are completed.

"At Pittsburg we noticed a custom of selling horses (common in the Western States:) if a man wishes to sell one, he rides up and down the market and streets, showing his paces, and starts it, say 20 dollars, calling out, as he rides along, 'Twenty dollars! twenty dollars! and a capital one to rack,' &c.—(racking is a favourite ambling pace.) When he gets a fresh bid, he announces it: the last bidder has the horse. If the owner does not approve of being his own auctioneer, it is done by one of the city officers for a small premium.

"Our afternoon's ride was through the woods, where we saw many tracks of deer: one noble buck passed us within gun shot at an easy trot.

We observed several hunters' and travellers' encampments during the day; they are chosen on an elevated spot of ground, and poles, sticks, and branches, are constructed very roughly into a temporary hut. Mr. Keenan, where we breakfasted, tells us he can always buy a deer's carcase, even if it weighs a hundred weight, for a dollar, and the skin is worth as much more. He says, some of the expert hunters will kill 70 or 80 in a season, besides bears, wolves, foxes, turkeys, and other game: buffaloes, elks, and moose, used to be common here, but they have lately emigrated across he Mississippi and Ohio: beavers have also disappeared.

"In the afternoon we passed a party of about a hundred young men and women holding a barbecue frolic. It consists of a dinner, in which a roasted hog, in the Indian style, is the prominent article; and after it, dancing, wrestling, jumping, squirrel-shooting, &c. Where they all came from, seemed to be the wonder, as we had hardly seen a house the last ten miles.

"From the rascality and quarrelsome behaviour of a few of the Kentucky men, the whole people have got a very bad character amongst the sister states, especially for blackguardism, and their manner of fighting, when intoxicated; but this is certainly confined to the lowest, and is optional to the fighters. The question is generally asked—'Will you fight fair, or take it rough and tumble? I can whip you either way, by G——d!' The English reader knows what fair fighting is, but can have little idea of rough and tumble; in the latter case, the combatants take advantage, pull, bite, and kick, and with hellish ferocity strive to gouge, or turn each other's eyes out of their sockets. I never saw a gouging match, and though often of necessity in the lowest company, never had any one offer to do me that favour. I believe it is not so common by any means as is represented. I saw but two men who had been injured by this method of fighting—one had almost lost an eye, and the other, a free negro, was nearly or totally sightless. They both lived on the banks of the Ohio, where this dreadful art is most practised; it was introduced from the Southern states. There certainly ought to be a strong law enacted to prevent a resort to so brutal a practice; surely it is a disgrace and stigma to the legislature. Prize-boxing is unknown in the United States."

DUKE OF WELLINGTON AND THE SHEPHERD.

In the year 1818, as the Duke was upon a sporting visit at the seat of the marquis of Salisbury, Hatfield, he met with the following curious adventure.

A farmer who had been much annoyed by the hunters riding across his corn, directed his shepherd to stake up and make fast all his gates that adjoin the roads. It so happened that the Duke rode up to one of these gates, which the shepherd was lolling over, and who was directed by the Duke to open the gate for him. The shepherd refused compliance, and told him to go round, for he should not ride over his master's corn. The Duke therefore rode off. When the man went home, his master inquired of him if he had stopped the hunters? "Ay, master," the shepherd answered, "that I have—and not only them, but also that soldier-man that Bonaparte could not stop." The farmer took an early opportunity of apologizing to Lady Salisbury for the rudeness of his servant, and stated, that had he been aware that the Noble Duke would have been out that day, his gates should not have been fastened, and at the same time mentioned what his man had said, which on being related to the Duke, caused, as may be expected, a hearty laugh.

AN EPITAPH.

Beneath this turf a female lies,
  That once the boast of fame was;
Have patience, reader, if you're wise,
  You'll then know what her name was.

In days of youth, (be censure blind)
  To men she would be creeping;
When 'mongst the many one prov'd kind,
  And took her into—keeping.

Then to the stage* she bent her way,
  Where more applauded none was;

---

* A little spaniel bitch strayed into the Theatre, in Drury-Lane, and fixed upon Mr. Beard as her master and protec-

She gain'd new lovers ev'ry day,
  But constant still to—one was.

By players, poets, peers, address'd,
  Nor bribe nor flattery mov'd her;
And tho' by all the men caress'd,
  Yet all the—women lov'd her.

Some kind remembrance then bestow
  Upon the peaceful sleeper;
Her name was *Phillis*, you must know,
  One *Hawthorn* was her keeper.

MAJOR TOPHAM,
Of the Wold Cottage, Yorkshire.

Every public character who has in the least degree contributed towards the wellbeing of society merits some notice to posterity; and few are there to be found who have performed a more active part than the subject of the present memoir, either in fashionable life, or in the more healthful and invigorating pursuits of the sports of the field.

Major Edward Topham is the son of Francis Topham, Esq. LL.D. who was master of the faculties and judge of the perogative court of

---

tor, was constantly at his heels, and attended him on the stage in the character of Hawthorn. She died much lamented, not only by her master, who was a member of the *Beef Steak Club*, but by all the members; at one of their meetings, as many as chose it, were requested to furnish, at the next meeting an epitaph. Among divers, preference was given to the above, from the pen of the late worthy John Walton, to whom the club were obliged for the well-known ballad of "Ned and Nell," and some beautiful songs.

York, at which place he resided. He was reckoned one of the most eminent civilians of his day; and it was in a great measure owing to the number of unfortunate cases that came before him as a judge, which he so strongly represented in a phamphlet addressed to the then Lord Hardwicke, that the act which put an end to the Fleet marriages passed.

Major Topham passed eleven years at Eton, where he was fortunate enough to be distinguished by frequently having his verses publicly read by the master in school, or, as it is there termed, by being "sent up for good."

After leaving Eton, Major Topham went as a fellow-commoner to Trinity College, Cambridge, where he remained four years, long enough to put on what is there called "an Harry Soph's gown," which many people would think was exchanging a good for a bad gown; that of the fellow-commoner being purple and silver, and the Harry Soph black silk.

From Cambridge he went abroad for a year and a half, and afterwards travelled through Scotland. This little tour became better known, as he afterwards gave an account of it in "Letters from Edinburgh," published by Dodsley. As the work of a stripling, they were so well received, that the first edition was soon out of print. Thence he removed to the seat of all human joy, in the eyes of a young man, London, and entered into the first regiment of life-guards. He was soon appointed adjutant of that corps, and shortly after exhibited as a character in the windows of all the print shops, under the title of "The Tip-top Adjutant." In truth, he was a Martinette of his day, and shortly converted a very heavy ill-disciplined regiment into a very good one. In consequence of this he received several commendatory notices from the King, and the old general officers of the time.

The Major, however, was not so absolutely absorbed in military tactics, as even then totally to estrange himself from literary pursuits. In the midst of his various avocations, he wrote many prologues and epilogues, to the dramatic pieces of his friends. To some of Mr. Cumberland's dramatic pieces, and to all those composed by his friend Mr. Andrews, he gave the last word in the shape of an epilogue. Amongst those that produced the greatest applause on the stage, was a prologue spoken by Mr. Lee Lewis, in the character of Moliere's old woman, which had the effect of bringing for many nights together a full house before the beginning of the play—a circumstance in dramatic story somewhat singular.

The managers of Drury-lane, who had protracted their season to a great length, at the close of it, to add to their profits, let their theatre for a few nights to a party, collected, heaven knows how! of people who fancied they had great stage talents. Hamlet's advice to actors formed no part of their tragedy. Amongst the rest was the father of Lawrence the painter, who having been unsuccessful in the wine trade, as an innkeeper, fancied that he had, at least, all the spirit necessary for a tragedian.

It was this subject, luckily occurring at the time, that Major Topham selected for an epilogue, which was most admirably delivered by Miss Farren. The effect was such, that the elder Colman often declared that it brought five hundred pounds to the Haymarket theatre during that season.

Major Topham remained adjutant of the first life-guards about seven years, during which period he succeeded in making it the pattern regiment of the kingdom, and therefore, in some measure, actually merited the appellation of the Tip-top Adjutant. After this, in the regular course of purchase and promotion, he rose to be a captain.

At this time he first became acquainted with old Mr. Elwes, who frequently used to dine with him on guard, when he was not engaged in the House of Commons. The son of Mr. Elwes was at that time in the same regiment; and it was from this circumstance that Major Topham became enabled to confer on that son those essential benefits which he afterwards performed. Having great influence with old Elwes, he had often been solicited by his friend to take an opportunity of speaking to the father on the subject of making a will, as, from being a natural son, he could not have inherited without it. The repugnance to talking about his property, much more to disposing of it, was in Mr. Elwes inconceivable; and therefore it was a matter of the utmost delicacy and difficulty. Major Topham, however, was fortunate enough to choose a moment, and to find a way to overcome this difficulty, and the two sons owe entirely to him the whole of the immense property they now possess, and when perhaps this property may be estimated at seven hundred thousand pounds, it must be considered as a service, in point of importance, that has seldom been performed by one person to another.

From being more of a literary man than in general falls to the lot of officers, he had frequently at his dinner parties on guard, men not usually seen in a military mess. Horne Tooke, the elder Colman, M. P. Andrews, John Wilkes and many other characters then well known, were in the habit of visiting him there.

The life of a captain of horse-guards, except when on duty, which was only four days in every month, was, at that time, a life of perfect inactivity, and therefore soon became irksome to Major Topham.

A circumstance happened about this time to

the Major, which, as has been said, gave a sort of distinguishing colour to his future life. Mrs. Wells, of Drury-lane theatre, confessedly one of the most beautiful women of the day in which she lived, through the medium of a friend, sent to request him to write her an epilogue for her benefit. He naturally did not deny her request; and of course the reading and instructing her in the delivery, produced interviews, which the company of a woman so beautiful must always make dangerous. There are, as Sterne says, " certain chords, and vibrations, and notes, that are correspondent in the human feelings, which frequent interviews awaken into harmony," and—if puns did not require spelling —frequently produce a consort.

It may also be naturally supposed, that in return for the greatest gift a man can receive, the heart of a most beautiful woman, he would devise every method to become serviceable to her interests and dramatic character, and think his time and talents never better employed than in advancing the reputation of her he loved. This desire, indeed, gave a new spur to his mind, and a fresh activity to his genius. It was this idea that first inspired the thought of establishing a public print. It has been said, more than metaphorically, that "Love first created the world." Here it was realized. Gallantry began what literature supported, and politics finished. It was thus, as we understand, from a wish to assist Mrs. Wells in her dramatic life, that the paper of "The World" first originated, and which, beginning from the passion for a fine woman, attracted to itself shortly afterwards as much public notice as ever fell to the share of a daily, and constantly a very fugitive publication.

From the dispositions he made, perhaps more from the conversation which was generally held that such a publication was about to come forth, in one week the demand for The World exceeded that which had been made in the same time for any other newspaper. With the exception of the Anti-Jacobin, no public print ever went upon the same ground; not depending so much on the immediate occurrence or scandal of the day, as upon the style of writing, and the pleasantries that appeared there. In truth, some of the most ingenious men contributed towards it; and when the names of Merry, Jerningham, Andrews, Mrs. Cowley, Mrs. Robinson, Jekyll, and Sheridan, are mentioned as having frequently appeared in this print, the remark will not be doubted. The poetry of The World was afterwards collected in four volumes. Merry and Mrs. Cowley were the Della Crusca, and Anna Matilda, who were so long admired, and who, during the whole writing of those very beautiful poems, were perfectly unknown to each other.

But admired as these productions, and many

others were, that appeared in the paper of The World, it is a singular fact that the correspondence of two boxers, Humphries and Mendoza, raised the sale of the paper in a higher degree than all the contributions of the most ingenious writers. It was the fashion of that time for the pugilists to send open challenges to each other, and thus publicly announce their days of fighting. This they chose to do through "The World," as considering it the most fashionable paper.*

In a short time Mrs. Wells, by her own intrinsic merit, added to a little instruction, rose to be one of the first actresses of her time.

Major Topham's wishes, therefore, were fully gratified. The paper of The World, of which he was editor, had extended itself beyond his utmost expectations. It was looked to as a repository for all the best writers of the day; it gave the tone to politics, and what to him was still dearer, it contributed to the fame of the woman he loved.

But alas! the dearest and most sanguine of our hopes are but as breath. Mrs. Wells, in her eagerness to appear in a particular part, to oblige the manager of Covent-garden, too soon after the birth of her last child, produced a re-

* Bell's Weekly Despatch is now the vehicle for these curious literary compositions.

volution of milk, which afterwards flew to her head, and occasionally disordered her brain.

On this melancholy event taking place, the paper of The World, at which Major Topham, had incessantly laboured for nearly five years, and which had now attained an unrivalled degree of *eminence*, lost in his eyes all its charms. He first determined to let it, reserving a certain profit from its sale; and in a short time he resolved to dispose of it altogether.

In fact, and without a pun, on quitting " The World," Major Topham retired to his native county, where the duties a country magistrate, in a large county, occupied his time, added to a farm of some hundred acres under his own management.

Major Topham, living in the Wolds of Yorkshire, has not been insensible to the pleasure derived from rural sports. Among other country amusements, he has founded many coursing establishments. He was the possesser of the celebrated greyhound Snowball, brother to Major, the property of Colonel Thornton—whose breed is so well known, and so highly esteemed in the Sporting World. The daughters of Major Topham are greatly distinguished for their superior skill in horsemanship.

One of the last of his literary works was the life of Mr. Elwes. If wide spread circulation be any test of merit, it certainly had this to boast. It was originally published in numbers in The World, which it raised in sale one thousand papers. It was thence copied into all the different provincial ones, and afterwards with some revisions, collected and published in a volume. It has gone through eleven editions. The late Horace Walpole used to say of it, that it was the best collection of genuine anecdote he knew.

Nor has this author been less distinguished for his knowledge and experience as a sportsman, having very handsomely contributed his assistance in writing an interesting account of "ancient and modern coursing," also interesting notes to a new and beautiful edition of Somerville's chase.*

No man has more of the manners of a gentleman, or more of the ease and elegance of fashionable life, than Major Topham; though fond of retirement, his knowledge of life and manners enlivens his conversation with a perpetual novelty, while his love of humour and ridicule, always retained within the bounds of benevolence and good-nature, add to the pleasures of the social table, and animate the jocundity of the festive board.

* Published by Sherwood, Neely, and Jones, price 6s. with some fine engravings by Scott.

ON VIEWING AN OLD BENCH IN THE PARK AT WINDSOR, AFTER AN ABSENCE OF THIRTY YEARS.

By Major Topham.

Hail, *good old bench!* the seat of my first folly,
Thy sight creates a smile, and makes me melancholy:
   For oh! what years have roll'd between,
   How many a tragic, comic scene,
   Since sporting on thy playful green,
Thames saw me first—an ETON BOY.
   Dear scenes of fond illusion past,
   Too gay, too innocent to last!
But thou, rude bench, of pleasant seeming,
But with disaster strangely teeming:
   For reckless he who venturing first
   On that strange land with witchery curst,
   Where magic visions strike the eyes,
   But WOMAN in the ambush lies.
   —Woman to harm and to annoy—
   The source of every tear and every joy!

Then stop forewarn'd—a moment stop from sinning,
Thou dream'st not of the plagues but now beginning;
   Attracted by the dimpled smile,
   So playful and so free from guile,
   Yet so deceitful all the while.
Stop, while thou canst, *unthinking boy!*
   Mirthful have been thy days till now;
   Soon wilt thou wear an alter'd brow:
   Then wilt thou wonder that to-morrow
   So soon can wear the face of sorrow,
   Regret, distrust, and jealous fears,—
   For love, like rainbows, smiles in tears;
   Dewy and light his airy form.
   Then comes behind that April storm,
   WOMAN—to charm and to annoy,
   The source of every tear and every joy!

Then blest the hour, when time in pity cooling
The feverish vein, which leads us on to fooling,

And (be the tempter maid or wife)
Lures us to combat care and strife,
And break the bonds of social life:
'Till age arrests the infuriate boy;
Then comes *Reflection*, sober power,
Friendship, to charm the calmer hour,
A tie which knows not to disorder
With transports which on anguish border;
But cheers us like the setting sun—
When love his flaming course has run,
'Till every fond delusion o'er,
Deceitful woman charms no more,
WOMAN, to harm and to annoy,
The source of every tear, and every joy!

UNITED EFFORTS OF A PEDESTRIAN AND A HORSE.

At Chelmsford in Essex, in 1818, Mr. Ives, a resident, and a mare, belonging to Mr. Crooks, jun. sheep-dealer, also of Chelmsford, commenced the extraordinary undertaking of performing 200 miles in twenty-four hours. The mare and the pedestrian started at a quarter past one o'clock from the Red Lion, at Springfield; the former travelling six miles, and the latter one mile on the Colchester road. The mare performed sixty miles by ten o'clock at night, when she was taken into the stable and rested for four hours, after which she resumed her task, and had completed 132 miles by 43 minutes past 12 o'clock next day. The pedestrian, in the course of the night, rested three hours, and by half-past 12 o'clock the next day had made good seventy miles, which added to those performed by the mare, made 202 miles in twenty-three hours and twenty eight minutes, leaving thirty-two minutes to spare, and two miles over. The mare was led throughout her journeys by the proprietor and some of his friends, who occasionally relieved each other; and at the termination of her performance, appeared but very little, if at all, distressed, considering the extraordinary number of miles she had travelled. The pedestrian accomplished his part with apparent ease, and there is no doubt that they could have effected some miles in addition within the given time. Thousands of persons witnessed the result of this match against time, and at the conclusion the victors were escorted into Chelmsford by a considerable body of horsemen and a band of music.

ANIMALS, BIRDS, AND FOWLS, SPORTING, RACES, &c. AMONG THE AFGHAUNS.

By the Hon. Mountstuart Elphinstone.

The distant and extensive kingdom of Caubul, bounded on the east by Hindostan, on the south by the Persian gulf, and on the west by a desert, contains some animals apparently of a species distinct from those of other parts. The dogs, the Honourable Mountstuart Elphinstone, in his account of that kingdom, remarks, deserves to be mentioned. The greyhounds are excellent; they are bred in great numbers, particularly among the pastoral tribes, who are most attached to hunting. Pointers resembling our own in shape and quality, are by no means uncommon, and are called khundee. A long-haired species of cats, called boorank, are exported in great numbers, and are every where called Persian cats.

There are two or three sorts of eagles, and many kinds of hawks, among which is the gentle falcon, the best of all; the large gray short-winged bird, called bauz in Persian, and kuzzil in Turkish, is thought to be the goss-hawk. The shauheen is taught to soar over the falconer's head, and strike the quarry as it rises. The chirk is taught to strike the antelope, fasten on its head, and retard it till the greyhounds come up. Herons, cranes, and storks, are common, and also a bird, called cupk by the Persians and Afghauns, and the hill chicore by the Indians, but which is known in Europe by the name of the Greek partridge. A smaller bird, called soosee, it is said, has never been heard of but among the Afghauns. The favourite amusement of these people is the chase, which is followed in various modes, according to the nature of the country, and the game to be pursued. Large parties often assemble on horseback, or on foot, and form a crescent, which, sweeping the country to a very great extent, is sure to rouse whatever game may be in their range. They manage so as to drive it into a valley, or some other convenient place, when they close in, and fall upon it with their dogs and their guns. Still more frequently a few men go out together, with their greyhounds and their guns, to course hares, foxes, and deer, or shoot any game that may fall in their way.

In some parts of the country they take hares, or perhaps rabbits, with ferrets. Their mode of shooting deer is by stalking bullocks and camels, trained to walk between them and the game, so as to conceal the hunter. In winter they track wolves and other wild animals in the snow, and shoot them in their dens. In some places they dig a hole in the ground near the spring, and conceal themselves there to shoot the deer and other animals that come there at night to drink. They also go out at night to shoot hyænas, which then issue from their dens and prowl about for their prey. They never shoot birds flying, but fire at them with small shot as they are sitting or running along the ground. They have no hawking, except in the east; but often ride down partridges in a way which is much easier of execution than one would imagine. Two or more horsemen put up a partridge, which makes a short fly and sits down; a horseman then puts it up again, and the hunters relieve one another so as to allow the bird no rest till it becomes too tired to fly, when they ride over it as it runs, or knock it down with sticks.

Races are not uncommon, especially at marriages: the bridegroom gives a camel to be run for; twenty or thirty horses start, and they run for ten or twelve miles over the best ground they can find. With the better sort, it is a common amusement to tilt with their lances in the rest, at a wooden peg stuck in the ground, which they endeavour knock over, or to pick up on the point of their spears. They also practise their carbines and matchlocks on horseback; and all ranks fire at marks with guns, or with bows and arrows. They shoot for some stake; commonly for a dinner; but never for a large sum of money. The great delight of all the western Afghauns is to dance the attam or ghoomboor. From ten to twenty men or women stand up in a circle, (in summer before their houses and tents, and in winter round a fire,) a person stands within the circle to sing and play on some instrument. The dancers go through a number of attitudes and figures, shouting, clapping their hands, and snapping their fingers. Every now and then they join hands and move slow or fast, according to the music, all joining in chorus.

Most of their games appeared to the English very childish, and can scarcely be reconciled to their long beards and grave behaviour. Marbles are played by grown up men through all the Afghaun country and Persia. A game generally played, is one called khogsye by the Dooraunces, and cabuddee by the Tanjcks. A man takes his left foot in his right hand and hops about on one leg, endeavouring to overset his adversary, who advances in the same way. This is played by several on a side, and to a stranger appears very complicated. Quoits, played with circular flat stones; and hunt the slipper, played with a cap, are also very common; as are wrestling, and other trials of strength and skill.

Fighting quails, cocks, dogs, rams, and even camels, are much admired. During their rutting season, if camels are matched, they fight with such fury that the spectators are obliged to stand out of the way of the beaten camel, who runs off at his utmost speed, and is often pursued by the victor to a distance from the field of battle. All these games are played for some stake, sometimes for money, and sometimes the winner takes the beaten cock, ram, or camel; but the general stake is a dinner.

It would take a great deal of time to describe their gymnastic exercises, or the innumerable postures which wrestlers are taught to assume. Some of the principal we may, however, notice: In one of them the performer places himself on his hands and toes, with his arms stiff and his body horizontal, at a distance from the ground. He then throws his body forward, and at the same time bends his arms, so that his chest and belly almost sweep the ground. When his body is as far thrown forward as possible, he draws it back to the utmost; straightens his arms, and is prepared to repeat the motion. A person unused to this exercise could not perform it ten times without intermission: but such is the strength it confers when often used, that one English officer was able to go through it six hundred times without stopping, and this operation he repeated twice a day.

Another exercise is whirling a heavy club round the head, in a way that requires the exertion of the whole body. It is either done with an immense club held in both hands, or with one small club in each. A third exercise is to draw a very strong bow, which has a heavy iron chain instead of a ring. It is first drawn with the right hand like a common bow, then thrown over to the right, drawn with the left hand, and afterwards pulled down violently with both, till the head and shoulders appear between the bow and the chain. This last exercise only operates on the arms and the chest, but the others strain every muscle in the frame. There are many other exercises intended to strengthen the whole, or particular parts of the body, which a judicious master applies according to the defects of his pupil's formation. The degree to which these exercises bring out the muscles, and increase the strength, is not to be believed. Though fatiguing for the first few days, they afterwards occasion a pleasurable feeling, and a sensation of lightness and alacrity which lasts the whole day; and Mr. Elphinstone adds, "I never saw a man who had performed them long, without a large chest, fine limbs and swelling muscles. They are one of the best inventions which Europe could borrow from the East; and, in fact, they bear a strong resemblance to the gymnastic exercises of ancient Greece."

SAGACITY OF THE HEDGE-HOG.

During the summer of 1818, as Mr. Lane, game-keeper to the Earl of Galloway, was passing by the wood of Calscadden, near Garliestown, in Scotland, he fell in with a hedge hog, crossing the road at a small distance before him, carrying on its back six pheasant's eggs, which, upon examination, he found it had pilfered from a pheasant's nest hard by. The ingenuity of the creature was very conspicious, as several of the remaining eggs were holed, which must have been done by it, when in the act of rolling itself over the nest, in order to make as many adhere to its prickles as possible. After watching the motions of the urchin for a short time longer, Mr. Lane saw it deliberately crawl into a furze bush, where its nest was, and where the shells of several eggs were strewed around, which had, at some former period, been conveyed thither in the same manner.

Another instance of the sagacity of the hedge hog is also recorded by Plutarch:—"A citizen of Cyzicus formerly acquired the reputation of a good mathematician, for having learned the property of a hedge-hog. It has its burrows open in divers places, and to several winds; and foreseeing the change of the wind, stops the hole on that side; which that citizen perceiving, gave the city certain predictions to what corner the wind would shift next."

THE LAP DOG.
By W. Upton.

'Tis little *Shock*, my lady's dog,
   An angry bard expresses;
With curly charms must fill her arms,
   And share her fond caresses.

Dear woman! turn your eyes around,
   Another *Dog* implores ye;
Be not so blind, in man you'll find
   A creature that adores ye.

Nor spaniel, poodle, shock, or pug,
   (However they may grumble;)
To gain that bliss, from you a kiss,
   Were ever yet so humble.

Then ladies, dear ones! kinder grow,
   Nor live to teaze and flout him;
But make your plan that lap dog, *Man!*
   And *throw your arms about him.*

CURIOUS ACCOUNT OF A TAME SEAL.

In January, 1819, in the neighbourhood of Burntisland, a gentleman completely succeeded in taming a seal; its singularities attracted the curiosity of strangers daily. It appeared to possess all the sagacity of the dog, and lived in its master's house, and eat from his hand. In his fishing excursions, this gentleman generally took it with him, upon which occasions it afforded no small entertainment. When thrown into the water, it would follow for miles the track of the boat, and although thrust back by the oars, it never relinquished its purpose. Indeed it struggled so hard to regain its seat, that one would imagine its fondness for its master had entirely overcome the natural predilection of its native element.

THE SCORPION.
From Pananti's Account of Algiers.

The natives frequently amuse themselves by a curious kind of warfare, which is created by shutting up a scorpion and a rat together in a close cage, when a terrible contest ensues, which has been known to continue sometimes for above an hour; it generally ends by the death of the scorpion; but in a little time after, the rat begins to swell, and in violent convulsions soon shares the fate of his vanquished enemy. It is also a favourite diversion with the Moors, to surround one of these reptiles with a circle of straw, to which fire is applied; after making several attempts to pass the flames, it turns on itself, and thus becomes its own executioner.*

THE CLOWN AND THE GEESE.

In the beginning of July 1818, a gentleman, on his way by water from Westminster at

* In the "*Giaour*" this singular fact is finely alluded to, by Lord Byron.

Blackfriar's bridge, felt his curiosity excited by observing the craft which line the river on both sides, crowded with spectators, gazing with anxious eyes at some object on the surface of the water. Upon advancing a little nearer to the object of curiosity, he beheld a human being seated in a washing-tub, floating with the tide under the pilotage of six geese, yoked to the aquatic vehicle, and proceeding with all the grave composure of a civic voyage to Westminster. Whenever the geese were inclined to deviate, he observed they were gently guided by the aid of a stick into the right course again. On inquiring into the cause of this exhibition, he found that the personage thus launched upon so perilous an enterprise, was Usher, the professional grimacier of the Coburg theatre, whose aquatic feats of this description had acquired him much celebrity, and who, on this occasion, had laid a wager of ten guineas to perform a voyage from Blackfriars to Westminster, in the frail bark which we have just described.

THE CHASE OF LIFE.
By Mr. Upton.

The Age is a *Chase*, from the time we draw breath,
  The present, the future, and past;
And tho' all must yield to the grand archer, Death,
  The sport is kept up to the last.

The *Statesman's* a Huntsman, ambition's his *game*;
  The *Soldier* for glory contends;

The *Sailor* for England emblazon's his fame,
  And ranks with her dearest of friends.

The *Patriot's* a Lion, his country the field.
  He chooses to run down her foes;
The *Courtier's* a Spaniel, will supple and yield,
  And a *Coxcomb's* a Jay in fine clothes.

The *Bailiff's* a Kite, ever bent on his prey;
  The *Bully's* a Magpie, all talk;
The *Miser* a Muckworm, appears night and day,
  And a *Lawyer's* a blood-sucking *Hawk*.

The *Prude* is a Fox, rather crafty and sly,
  Pretending aversion to sin;
The *Coquet's* an Eel, that demands a sharp eye,
  And frequently not worth a pin.

The *Wife*, loving wife, is the pride of the *Chase*,
  And life's gloomy evening cheers;
And where is the *Hunter* can't easily trace,
  The sweet temper'd girls are all *Deers*.

THE HORSE AND VIPER.

The great viper called *Fer de Lance*, is one of the most dreadful scourges in the West Indies, but it is found only in Martinique, St. Lucia, and another small Island. This viper is so savage, that the moment it sees any person, it immediately erects itself, and springs upon him. In raising itself, it rests upon four equal circles formed by the lower part of the body; when it springs, these circles are suddenly dissolved. After the spring, if it should miss its object, it may be attacked with advantage; but this requires considerable courage, for, as soon as it can erect itself again, the assailant runs the greatest risk of being bitten. Often, too, it is so bold as to follow its enemy by leaps and bounds, instead of fleeing from him; and it does not cease the pursuit till its revenge is glutted. In its erect position it is so much the more formidable, because it is as high as a man, and can even bite a person on horseback.

M. Morreau de Jonnes was once riding through a wood, when his horse reared; and when the rider looked round to discover the cause of the animal's terror, he perceived a Fer de Lance viper standing quite erect in a bush of bamboo, and heard it hiss several times. He would have fired at it with his pistol, but the affrighted horse drew back so ungovernably, that he was obliged to look about for somebody to hold him. He now espied, at some distance, a negro upon the ground, wallowing in his blood, and cutting with a blunt knife the flesh from the wound occasioned by the bite of the same viper. When M. Jonnes acquainted him with his intention of killing the serpent, he earnestly opposed it, as he wished to take it alive, and make use of it for his cure, according to the superstitious notions of the negroes. He presently arose, cut some lianes, made a snare with them, and then concealing himself behind the bush, near the viper, he attracted its attention by a low whistling noise, and suddenly throwing a noose over the animal, drew it tight, and secured his enemy. M. Morreau saw this negro a twelvemonth afterwards, but he had not perfectly recovered the use of the limbs bitten by the viper. The negroes persecute these vipers with the greatest acrimony. When they have killed one, they cut off its head, and bury it deep in the earth, that no mischief may be done by the fangs, which are dangerous after the death of the animal. Men and beasts shun this formidable reptile; the birds manifest the same antipathy for that as they do for owls in Europe, and a small one of the Loxia kind, even gives warning by its cry, that a viper is at hand.

SKETCH OF A DISTINGUISHED SPORTSWOMAN.

Lady Fearnought was the only child of a gentleman of large fortune, in Sussex, who was a perfect Nimrod in the chase; he was doatingly fond of her. Having no son to initiate into his favourite pursuits, or participate with him in the pleasures of hunting and shooting, and seeing his daughter a fine robust girl, he determined to bring her up in the place of one; and, as she had strong animal spirits, great muscular strength, and rude health, she preferred partaking of the field sports of her father, to the lessons of the French governess and dancing-master, or being confined to work at the tambour-frame of her mother; in spite of whose gentle remonstrances, Mr. Beagle, aided by the inclinations of his romping daughter, vowed he would have his plan of education adopted.

In consequence at fifteen, she would take the most desperate leaps, and clear a five-barred gate with the keenest fox-hunter in the county. She was always in at the death : was reckoned the best shot within a hundred miles ; for having once levelled her death-dealing tube, the fate of the feathered tribe was inevitable, as the spoils she exultingly displayed sufficiently testified, when she turned out her net to her admiring father.

At seventeen, Emma Beagle, early habituated to exercise, had never felt the baleful curse of ill-health, that extermination of every comfort. Her height was five feet eight ; her person finely formed ; she had a commanding and majestic appearance. From the freedom of her education which had banished mauvaise honte, she had acquired a firm tone of voice, an impressive manner of delivering her sentiments, which, if it did not always carry conviction to her auditors, helped to awe them into silence. Her complexion was that of a bright brunette ; on her cheeks glowed the rich tints of health, laid on by Aurora, as she hailed the rosy-fingered goddess's approach on the upland lawn. Her eyes were of the darkest hazel, full of fire and intelligence ; her nose Grecian ; her hair a glossy chestnut, which flowed in luxuriant profusion upon her fine formed shoulders, in all its native graces, as she never would consent to its being tortured into the fantastic forms dictated by the ever-varying goddess, Fashion, to her votaries.

Her mind partook of the energies of her body, it was strong, nervous and masculine; she had a quick perception of character, and a lively wit, which she expressed in flowing and animated language; unused from early life to restraint, she never could be induced to put any on her words and actions, but had, to the present moment, done and said whatever struck her fancy, heedless of the world's opinion, which she treated with the most sovereign contempt.

At the period we have mentioned, she met at a fox chase, Sir Charles Fearnought, a handsome young man, just come of age, with whom she was charmed, by seeing him take a most desperate leap, in which none but herself had the courage to follow him. Mutually pleased with each other's powers, from that time they became constant companions, they hunted, shot, and played back-gammon together.

At this crisis the lovers were divided by Squire Beagle being ordered to Bath by his physician, after having had a severe fit of his old enemy the gout, in his stomach. To expel this foe to man from the seat of life to the extremities, he was sent to drink the waters of Bladud's fount, though in the squire's opinion, old Madeira would have been much more pleasant, and of equal utility; but the faculty persisted, and he was compelled to yield. He would no without his darling Emma—deprived of whose society he could not exist a single day.

This was Miss Beagle's first introduction to the fashionable world, except at an assize, a race, or an election ball. It was all, to her, new and wonderful; she was at first amused by the novelty and splendour of the gay city of Bath, that emporium of cards, scandal, and ceremony. With her ideas of free agency, she was soon disgusted with the painful restraint imposed on her by the latter; wild as the wind, and unconfined as air, she soon bid defiance to rule and order, determined to please herself, just as she used to do at Huntsman's Hall. In consequence of this wise resolve, she would mount her favourite blood-horse, gallop over Claverton Downs for a breathing before breakfast—leap off at the pump-room—dash in—charge up the ranks between yellow-faced spinters and gouty parsons, to the terror of the lame and decrepid—toss down a glass of water—quite forget the spur with which she rode—entangle it in the fringe of some fair Penelope's petticoat, who, in knotting it, had beguiled many a love-lorn hour, which this fair equestrian demolished in a moment, paying not the least attention to the comments her behaviour occasioned the company to make, such as—"How vastly disagreeable—monstrous rude—quite brutish—only a fit company for her father's hounds—I wonder how her mother, who is really a very polite bred woman, can think of letting her loose without a muzzle!" To audible whispers like these, Miss Beagle either laughed contemptuously, or, as her wit was keen and pointed, she made the retort courteous, and by her sarcasms soon silenced her antagonists.

At the balls she paid as little attention to precedence and order, as she did to ceremony in the pump-room. In vain the master of the ceremonies talked " about it, and about it ;" in vain he looked sour or serious. She laughed in his face—advised him to descend from his attitude, that only made him look queer and quizzical; then walked to the top of the room, and took her place upon those seats held sacred for nobility, that were not to be contaminated by plebeians. In vain the elected sovereign of etiquette talked of his delegated authority, and remonstrated against her encroachments, as indecorous and improper. The men supported her in all these freaks; the women, afraid of her satirical powers, only murmured their disapprobation.

The males were all charmed with the graceful beauty of her person, and the wild playful eccentricities of her manner: she was the toast and admiration of Bath, under the appellation of—" La Belle Savage."—The females concealed the envy they felt at this new rival of their charms, under a pretended disgust of her unfeminized manner, and masculine pursuits;

while she felt and expressed a perfect contempt of their trifling avocations, and used to say they were pretty automatons, whose minds were as imbecile as their persons.

Tired of the dull routine of fashionable follies, as the pleasure of surprising the crowd lost its novelty, Miss Beagle sighed for the time that was to restore her to her early habits. Of all the men that fluttered round, praised her charms, and vowed themselves her devoted adorers, she saw none that could stand in competition or dispute her heart with her favourite companion in the chase, the manly, bold, and adventurous Sir Charles Fearnought.

Her father, who, by drinking the waters, had expelled the gout from his stomach to his feet, and was content to accept a prolonged existence through the medium of excruciating torments, could not, till pronounced by the faculty to be in a state of convalescence, remove to Huntsman's Hall. Miss Beagle, obliged to remain in a place of which she was heartily tired, sought amusement in her own way, nor gave herself trouble what the company, with whom, to oblige her mother, she associated, thought of her actions.

At length Mr. Beagle, with his family, left Bath, and returned to Huntsman's Hall, where he soon received a visit from Sir Charles Fearnought, who made overtures to the old gentleman of marrying his blooming Emma. Mr.

Beagle discovered the pleasure with which she received the Baronet's proposal; accepted the offer with as much eagerness as it was made, by the intended son-in-law, and, as the estates joined, and their pursuits were so congenial, every one pronounced it a good match.

Soon after Sir Charles received the hand of the blooming Emma from her father; after which the new married pair, with a splendid retinue, set off for Partridge Lodge, the seat of Sir Charles, who, with the old-fashioned hospitality of his progenitors, ordered open house to be kept for his tenants and dependants. The October brewed at his birth, and preserved for this joyous occasion, was now poured out in liberal potations, and drank to the health of the bride and bridegroom; an ox was roasted whole in the park, and the plum-pudding of our hardy sires smoked on the festive board. This rural fete in the old English style, lasted a week.

Let us now follow Lady Fearnought, and note her entree into the great world, aided by the advantages of youth, beauty, fortune, fashion, and consequence, the admiration of the men, the envy of the women, and the gaze of the multitude. Through the entreaties and remonstrances of her husband and friends, she allowed herself to be presented at court, to have a box at the opera, and so far to comply with the fashionable circles, to which she had been introduced, as to attend their routs, and give them at her own house; but these were not the amusements congenial to her mind, and she determined that, as she yielded to her husband's inclinations in town, she would live to please herself in the country. For this purpose she kept a pack of fox hounds, that were reckoned the stanchest in the country; her stud was in the highest condition; her pointers excellent; and the partridges felt she had not forgot to take a good aim.

Obliged, by fashion's law, to pass some of the winter months in London every year, she soon threw off the restraint that tyrant custom imposes on the sex: amused herself by riding her favourite blood horse, Tarquin, against the male equestrians in Hyde-Park, or driving her phaeton, with four fleet coursers in hand, through the fashionable streets, turning a corner to an inch to the wonder and terror of her beholders. The ladies, who were constantly hearing her admired by the men for her prowess, and venturous feats of horsemanship, finding lady Fearnought was quite the rage, sickened with envy; determining, as they could not persuade her to follow their fashions, they would aspire to imitate hers.

From thence we may date the era of women venturing their pretty necks in a fox-chase, shooting flying, and becoming female charioteers, to rival the celebrity of the fair huntress, who was at the head of the haut-ton, with all these dashing ladies; and we had Fearnought riding hats, Fearnought boots and spurs, and Fearnought saddles!

When Lady Fearnought had been married about fourteen years, she had the misfortune to lose her husband, who was thrown from his horse during a fox-chase, and fractured his skull, by attempting a desperate leap. His beloved lady who had cleared it a few moments before, saw the accident, immediately sprung from her horse, and while she sent for a surgeon and a carriage, no house being near the spot where the accident happenned, she threw herself on the ground by his side, and laying his bleeding head on her lap, shed a torrent of genuine tears over the only man she ever loved. He was unable to speak, but seemed sensible of her tender sorrow; for he feebly pressed her hand, and before any assistance arrived he expired in her arms.

She mourned for him with unfeigned sorrow: "her occupation seemed to be gone;" her horses fed quietly in their stables, while for the space of three months the hounds slept in their kennels, and she wore a black riding habit for six. But time, which ameliorates the keenest anguish, and reconciles us to all things, aided by the conviction that we cannot recall the tenants of the tomb, failed not to pour its lenient balm into her wounded bosom; and Lady Fearnought "was herself again."

Sir Charles left an only son by this lady, the present Sir Henry Fearnought, who following the example of his father and mother, we see him now at the pinnacle of fashion, a Nimrod in the chase, a Jehu in London streets, a jockey riding his own matches at Newmarket, a bore at the opera, and a pigeon at the ladies' faro-tables! but he is a mixed character: he seeks celebrity by mixing with men of quality and fashion; to gain the reputation of being one himself, he imitates all their follies, though they are not the sort from which by inclination, he is enabled to receive any pleasure; for this he associates with the wives and daughters of needy nobility, with whom his money will compensate for his manners, though, did he give the sensations of his heart fair play, he would mix among the buxom daughters of his fox-hunting neighbours.

To gratify his desire for fame, he will draw straws for hundreds, race maggots for thousands: has a chariot built by Leader, in which he never rides; keeps an opera-dancer whom he seldom sees: but this is to give him eclat with the fashionable world, and stamp him as a man of high *ton!* for, to indulge his real taste, he steals in a hackney-coach to the embraces of his dear Fanny Frolic, once the dairy maid of his mother, but now his mistress, in a snug lodging in Mary-le-bone, whom he admires for the vulgar but native charms of rosy cheeks, white teeth, and arms as blue as a bilberry.

Lady Fearnought, his mother, at the present period is not yet forty, though she appears much older; for she is grown robust. Her complexion is died of the deepest bronze, occasioned by living so much on horseback, and exposing herself to the warring elements in all seasons; for the burning sun, or the pelting storm, deter her not from her accustomed avocations. By her management of herself she is so truly case-hardened, that she sets coughs, colds, and sore throats, at defiance!

She rises at daybreak, plunges directly into a cold bath, makes a meat breakfast, then mounts her fleet mare, and, according to the season, either hunts, shoots, or courses, till dinner. After having visited her stud, sits down to backgammon with the vicar; but if she has a visiter that can play, she prefers her favourite game, chess.

But though she has done every thing to preserve her health, and destroy her beauty, still she is a fine woman, and remains a favourite of the neighbouring gentlemen; is their companion in field sports, and often entertains with a dinner the members of the hunt in the vicinity.

SINGULAR CIRCUMSTANCE OF A BALL FOUND IN THE HEART OF A BUCK.

From the Edinburgh Medical and Surgical Journal.

A Buck that was remarkably fat and healthy in condition, in August, 1816, was killed in Bradbury Park; and on opening him it was discovered that, at some distant time he had been shot in the heart, a ball being found in a cyst in the substance of that viscus, about two inches from the apex. The surface of the cyst had a whitish appearance; the ball weighs two hundred and ninety-two grains, and was quite flat. Mr. Richardson, the park keeper, who opened the animal, is of opinion that the ball had struck some hard substance before entering the body of the deer. That the animal should subsist long after receiving this ball is endeavoured to be accounted for from the instance of a soldier who survived forty-nine hours after receiving a bayonet wound in the heart: however the recovery from a gun shot wound in an animal inferior to man can in no respect materially alter the importance of the fact, and of the great extent to which this vital organ may sustain an injury from external violence.

MY FANCY.

What is it that impels mankind
To stretch the procreative mind,
By this or that thing joy to find?
Fancy.

"What was it," dark-eyed Rosa cries,
"First made young Frederic charm my eyes,
And still, for still my fond heart sighs?"
My Fancy.

"What was it," questioning Charles exclaims,
"First lit the fire that wisdom blames,
And lovely woman still enflames?"
My Fancy.

What was it made my tongue so glib,
To bet on Scroggins, Ford, or Crib,
Where peers and blackguards swear and fib?
My Fancy.

What was it madly fired my brain,
To try the sportive "seven's the main,"
And curse the dice that threw in vain?
My Fancy.

What was it led my soul agog,
To range the meadows, hill and bog,
Delighted with my gun and dog?
My Fancy.

What call'd me up at break of morn,
To join the shrill mouth'd hounds and horn,
And shake the dew drops from the thorn?
My Fancy.

And now, to close this answering rhyme,
Bombastic, doggrel and *sublime!*
What is it whispers—and 'tis time?
My Fancy.

AN ACCOUNT OF THE DUTCH GAME OF KLOVEN.
From Mitchell's Tour through Belgium, Holland, &c.

A Traveller, who was at Leyden in the summer of 1816, observes, "There was one amusement I saw there, which we have not in England, which affords a most agreeable, gentle exercise, and is particularly adapted for a cold moist climate, which often denies enjoyments out of doors. It is called *Kloven*, and I shall here describe it as I saw it performed at a place of public entertainment, about a mile and a half without the Harlæm gate of Leyden, near the country-house where the great Boerhaave resided. There was a large room, about seventy feet long, and upwards of twenty broad. A walk along the side was partitioned off with boards, raised three feet high, and the rest of the room was laid with a whitish clay and sand, made very hard and smooth. About nine feet from each end of the room, in the exact middle, was a small pillar, the lower part of brass. There were two stuffed balls, rather hard, of the size of twelve pound cannon balls; and clubs, the lower parts of which were also of brass. Two people play; the first commences at one end of the room, and drives his ball towards the pillar at the other; the second player commencing at the same time, does the same to his ball. He of the two, whose ball has rolled nearest the pillar, has now the first blow. They strike their balls alternately, and the object is to make the ball roll first against one pillar, and then they drive it to the other end of the room, to try to make it strike the other pillar. He whose ball first does so, gains the first notch. The principle and mode of playing, bears a resemblance to the Scotch game of Golf. The exercise is gentle, and the game seems easy, but it requires considerable dexterity. The landlord charges nothing for the room, as the parties usually play for a bottle of wine; and it affords great entertainment to the lookers on, who also wish to be doing something for the good of the house."

THE CHAMOIS.
From "Alpine Sketches."

The Chamois is a little larger than a goat, but much superior in power and agility. The strongest man cannot hold one of a month old: they bound from precipice to precipice to a prodigious distance, gaining the loftiest summits, and precipitating themselves from the steepest rocks, without fear. The chase of this animal occupies a great part of this mountainous population, and many perish annually in the hazardous pursuit.

Often the hunter, overtaken by a dark mist, loses himself amongst the ices, and dies of cold and hunger; or the rain renders the rocks so slippery that he is unable to reascend them. In the midst of eternal snows, braving all dangers, they follow the Chamois frequently by the marks of their feet; when one is perceived at a distance, the hunter creeps along till within reach of his gun, which he rests on a rock, and is almost sure of his prey. Thus the innocent beast, which tranquilly feeds, perhaps enjoys the last moments of its happy existence. But if his watchful eye perceives the enemy, as is often the case, he flies from rock to rock, "timor addidit alas," and the fatigues of the pursuer begin, who traverses the snows, and climbs the precipices, heedless of how he is to return. Night arrives, yet the hopes of the morrow re-assure him, and he passes it under a rock. There, without fire, without light, he draws from his wallet a little cheese and oaten bread, which he is obliged to break with a stone, or with the hatchet he carries to cut his path in the ice. This repast finished, he falls asleep in his bed of snow, considering what route the Chamois has probably taken. At break of day he awakens, insensible to the charms of a beautiful morning, to the glittering rays which silver the snowy summits of the mountains around him, and thinking only of his prey, seeks fresh dangers. Thus they frequently remain many days in these horrible deserts, while their wives and families scarcely dare to sleep, lest they should behold the spirits of their dead husbands; for it is believed that a Chasseur, after his death, always appears to the person who is most dear to him, to make known where lie his mangled remains, to beg the rites of burial.

ACCOUNT OF HIGHLAND SPORTS,
Which took place at Strmidan Parry, Sept. 14, 1816.

At sunrise the standard waved on the old castle tower, but the inclemency of the preceding night and morning, retarded till ten the farther operations of the day: the scene was then opened by wall pieces, six and six, answering each other from "Cruganan Phithich," and the front of the Mansion-house; after which the whole mustered at Invergary to the pipe and clan banner; and thence countermarched to lodge those ancient family pieces in their armoury. They then proceeded to "Tomm na chouse," when, having halted, they were arranged like marshalled clansmen, (a detachment of the 78th Highlanders advancing in front to keep the ground clear,) and marched down on "Strmidan," the field sports, fording the waters in the good old Highland style. "Ann gualaidh a cheile!" and in this and the after proceeding of the day, the "Tuan Suidhe" was ably supported by "Cabber Feidh, the Mackenzie chief, and "Ard Tanistear Raonilich agus Clann Dhomuill," Colonel Macdonell of the Coldstream Guards, Captain Ross, Captain Macdonald (Glencoe,) with many other steady and respectable friends of this Institution. On entering the grounds, where tents had been previously pitched, and where the feast was soon to be spread in all the abundance and simplicity of the days of Ossian, neither was the blaze nor the songs of the bards forgot, while the feast of the shells circulated to "Comunnn nam fior Ghaidheal." "Tombac Mac Mhic Alastair" coursed here its welcome rounds; at proper intervals, to loyal, patriotic, and appropriate toasts succeeded "An Righ," "Ard Fhlath Comunn Ghaidhealach Lunnuin," &c. and the martial-toned bag pipe announced the opening of each game. "The field of mountain game, that brace the limbs, and fit for deeds of fame." And first the prize for ball-shooting was contended for, in which Glengarry, Allangrange, Colonel Macdonell of the Guards, C. B. K. M. T. and St. Wr. Captain Falconer, of the 79th Highlanders, and Capt. Morgan, distinguished themselves by breaking the target at about 120 yards. There appeared besides the "Cann Suidhe," three of the original winners at sharp shooting in the ground, viz. John Macdonell (Macalastair,) from Laddy; Hugh Macdonell (Macallan,) Balalistair; and Angus Mac Innes, from "Seann Talamh."

The foot race was then started (to run a distance of nearly five miles, the roads in many parts rough and unmade) by John Kennedy, " Mac Jan More," from Glengarry; Angus M'Eobhan, Rhuagha Kennedy, from Laggan; Archibald Macdonell, from Glenmorriston; and Ewen Kennedy, Mac Jan Mhic Eobhan, in which the two first were victorious, though the others did not want merit in the contest. Many gentlemen present spontaneously insisted upon contributing money to the winners, which was notified at starting, and won in able style, to the great delight of all on the spot.

The lifting of the stones was next resorted to, and was practised by the strong (in part) during the intervals of the runners' absence; in this, Serjeant Ranald Macdonell, "Na Craig," from Glengarry, maintained his original superiority with great ease; next Allan Macdonell, from Glenlee, carried it 42 yards: Donald Macdonell, from Lundy, 30 yards; John Macmaster, from Dockinassy, 28 yards and a half; John Chisholm, from Glenmorriston, 26 yards; Donald Cameron, from Dockinassy, 20 yards—several others who tried it, in vain, or declined having their names inserted, from the little hand they made of it, and the well authenticated efforts of John More Macdonell, late of Montcraggie, in Glengarry, and of James Macdonell, "Mac Fear Balemhian," from Abertarff, with this very stone, were listened to with pleasure by all, and astonishment by many. "Thig so agus theo u Feot," was now sounded for the Cearnach's feast, which consisted chiefly of beef, mutton, venison, broth, haggisses, &c. &c. after which the "Cuach" circulated again, and the games were resumed to the sound of the pipe.

Broadsword, cudgelling, and the dirk dance, had now been intended, but the unavoidable absence of two principal performers disappointed those hopes, one champion only of three being on the ground.

Putting the stone therefore succeeded, when Ranald Macdonell, "do Sbilochel Allan Mac Raonuill," from Leck of Glengarry, evinced his wonted superiority; among the others were observed Mr. George Macdonell, "au ceadna," Alexander Smith, gardener to Glengarry, and Alexander Grant, ploughman to Captain Morgan, the two last standing Putters.

The standing and running leap were denied us, from the shortness of the day, and heaving the sledge hammer was introduced in their room, than which few, if any of those manly games, the former pastime of Caledonians, show more the combined strength and activity of its performers. It calls forth every nerve in the human frame to its fullest pitch, and this, and putting the stone, were at all times favourites among our Highland ancestors. Here Sergeant Ranald Macdonell again maintained the superiority he had evinced for years back, as the Rae Highlanders, and his own regiment witnessed in a contest (during the Irish rebellion) with their companions.

Wrestling, pulling the stick, tossing the bar of iron, pitching the cabber, and several others, were among the Highland amusements of old, but the shortness of a most joyous and harmonious day forbade the entering upon either of them now. The sun being down, the gathering sounded afresh, and a dram being first circulated on the spot, the whole countermarched for

Glengarry House, where, after their "Deoch'n Doruis," the commoners, and those otherwise engaged, went to their various destinations, while the leaders of the party supped, and kept it up, bringing in the birth-day of Fear Bunch-hir with great glee in the true spirit of their hearts, before they retired to rest. An unavoidable circumstance (which, for the first time, prevented Mac Mhic Alastair's attendance at the last meeting of True Highlanders) delayed the timeous notice requisite for the more distant Highlanders and Isles; still the sports were very numerously attended, and such of the spectators as assumed the garb, met with every attention from the joyous Highlanders present.

MAJOR LEESON.

Few men experienced greater vicissitudes, or obtained more notoriety on the turf, than the above personage, who ultimately died in an obscure lodging, in the rules of the King's Bench. Those who have only heard of the irregularities of the latter days of the late Major, might suppose that silence would be the best tribute that could be paid to his memory. This consideration, however, would defeat the principal end of biography—instruction. Patrick Leeson, the subject of this sketch, was born at Nenagh, in the county of Tipperary, in the year 1754. It cannot be said that fortune smiled deceitful on his birth, for the wealth of his family consisted only of a few cows and horses, and a farm, on which three generations had subsisted with peace and competence.

Patrick's father had received an education beyond that of an husbandman, who was obliged to till the ground with his own hands; but as his sober wishes never strayed beyond the bounds of his own farm, he was at first determined that his son should tread in his own steps, and that he should not be spoiled by an education beyond his humble views. Patrick, however, was soon distinguished by a quickness of perception, and a promptitude of expression, beyond his years, and, in order that these qualities might be improved to a certain extent, he was sent to learn the Latin tongue, under the instruction of a relation, who looked upon all science and human excellence to be treasured up in that language, with which he was well acquainted, for he had made it his study from his boyish days up to his grand climacteric. Our young pupil made so rapid a progress in his grammar, that his preceptor and father began to conceive the highest hopes of his talents; and, as they were both very pious men, they thought such a star should shine only in the hemisphere of the church, to use the pedagogical expression.

Patrick, it seems, was not so deeply enamoured with abstinence and prayer, for he was already put upon this regimen: he thought that youth might indulge, without criminality, in some of those amusements which are peculiar to that season; such as dancing, wrestling, riding, &c. in each of which he excelled, nature having favoured him with a fine person, and a healthy constitution.

He had now nearly accompanied the prince of Roman historians through all his battles, sieges, &c. when a circumstance happened which put a stop to his classical career. A recruiting party came to Nenagh; "The ear-piercing fife, and the spirit-stirring drum" were not lost in such a buoyant mind, and Patrick protested that he would rather carry a musket as a private, than rule a score of parishes with the nod of a mitre. His grand uncle, a catholic priest, was consulted on the occasion. The good old man, after some consideration, gave it as his opinion, that his nephew was destined by nature to wear a red coat instead of a black one; and that examples were not wanting in his own family of those that had risen to unenvied honours in the tented field. Patrick's views were liberally seconded by a Scottish nobleman.

At the age of seventeen he came to London, as ignorant of the world as if he had just dropped into it. As he had spent, or rather wasted his time, to use his own phrase, in the study of words, he began to study things; for this purpose he was sent to Mr. Alexander's academy, at Hamstead, where, in a very short time, he laid in a tolerable stock of mathematical knowledge. He was now transplanted, through the munificence of his noble patron, to the celebrated academy of Angiers, in France, where he had the double advantage of finishing his military studies, and at the same time of learning the French language, which he spoke ever after with fluency. Whilst at this seminary he fought a duel with Sir W. M———; the courage exerted by these two gentlemen, on that occasion, has been always spoken of to the honour of both: He was soon after appointed a lieutenant in a regiment of foot, in which he conducted himself with the propriety of a man who considers the word soldier and gentleman as synonymous terms.

The only act of indiscretion that can be laid to his charge, if it can be called by that name, will find a ready apology in the impetuosity of youthful blood, and the affection he bore to every man in the regiment, which was reciprocal. The sergeant, a sober, steady man, was wantonly attacked by a blacksmith, who was the terror of the town. The sergeant defended himself as long as he was able, with great spirit, but was obliged, after a hard contest, to yield to his athletic antagonist. This intelligence reached Mr. Leeson's ears the next morning; without delay he set out in pursuit of the victor, whom he found boasting of the triumph he had gained over the lobster, as he called the sergeant. The very expression kindled Leeson's indignation into such a flame, that he aimed a blow at the fellow's temple, which he warded off, and returned with such force, that Leeson lay for some minutes extended on the ground. Leeson, however, renewed the attack; victory, for a considerable time, seemed to declare on the side of his antagonist; but as soon as the scale turned in favour of the lieutenant, he followed one blow after the other with such rapidity and success, that the son of Vulcan sunk at last, and yielded up the palm, with a copious effusion of blood, the loss of seven or eight teeth, and eyes beat to a jelly. In order to complete the triumph, Leeson placed him in a wheel-barrow, and in this situation he was wheeled through all the town, amidst the acclamations of the populace.

Soon after this, Mr. Leeson exchanged his lieutenancy for a cornetcy of dragoons. It may seem a little extraordinary, that a man who had escaped those snares that are strewed in the paths of youth, should fall into them at the time when prudence began to assume her influence over the heart. The gaming table now presented itself in all its seductive charms. He could not resist them: and an almost uninterrupted series of success led him to Newmarket, when his evil genius, in the name of good luck, converted him, in a short time, into a professed gambler. At one time he had a complete stud at Newmarket; and his famous horse, Buffer, carried off the capital plates for three years and upwards. As Leeson was a man of acute discernment, he was soon initiated into all the mysteries of the turf. He was known to all the black legs, and consulted by them on every critical occasion. Having raised an independent regiment, he was promoted to a majority. The Major, it was well known, was greatly indebted to the exertions of Courtenay, the celebrated Union Piper, for the rapidity with which he raised the above regiment. Courtenay was a choice spirit, and, like Morland, would sooner play on his pipes to amuse his poor countrymen, than gratify the wishes of noblemen, although handsomely paid for it. Courtenay resided at the house of rendezvous, where, the sweet strains of his pipes, added to copious draughts of whiskey, produced the complement of men in a few days. The period was so short, that Leeson won a great bet upon it. He continued for some time to maintain the dignity of his rank, and even expressed a wish to resume that conduct which had endeared him for many years to the good and the brave; but the temptations which gambling held out were too strong to be resisted, and a train of ill-luck preyed upon his spirits, soured his temper, and drove him to that last resource of an enfeebled mind—the brandy-bottle. As he could not shine in his wonted splendour, he sought the most obscure places in the purlieus of St. Giles's, where he used to pass whole nights in the company of his countrymen of the lowest, but industrious class, charmed with their songs and native humour. It is needless to point out the result of such a habit of life—Major Leeson, who was once the soul of whim and gaiety, sunk into a state of stupor and insensibility. On some occasions, it is true, he emerged from this state; but it was the emergency of a meteor that vanishes as it expands, and only left those that witnessed it, to lament the fall of a man who once promised to be an ornament to a profession that was dear to him in his last moments. Having contracted a number of debts, he was constantly pursued by the terriers of the law, and alternately imprisoned by his own fears, or confined in the King's Bench.

A few years since he married a Miss Mullet, who shared all his afflictions, and discharged all the duties of an affectionate wife. When sober, his manners were gentle and conciliating; and his conversation, on many occasions, evinced considerable mental vigour. He was generous and steady in his friendships, but the dupe of flattery. Having experienced all those vicissitudes attendant on a life of dissipation, he was sensible of the immediate approach of his dissolution, and talked of death as a friend that would relieve him of a load that was almost insupportable. He expired in the midst of a conversation with a few friends, and waved a gentle adieu with his hands, when he found that his tongue could not perform that office.

EPITAPH, ON A GREAT CARD PLAYER.

Will, in this world, had many a *rub* to tame
His spirits, yet he with his rubs was blest—
For cards were heaven—but now a *single* game,
Quite *grave and low*, he plays at endless whist.

His *hands* are chang'd, and all his *honours* gone;
He cannot call at *eight*, howe'er afraid;
His *suit* a shroud; his *sequence* to be shown,
Must wait untoll'd till the last *trump* is play'd.

MARKET FOR SINGING BIRDS DOGS, &c. IN RUSSIA.

From Clarke's Travels.

On a Sunday, in Moscow, the market is a novel and interesting spectacle from five in the morning till eight.—The Place de Gallitzin, a spacious area, near the Kremlin, is filled by a concourse of peasants, and people of every description, coming to buy or sell white peacocks, fan-tailed and other curious pigeons; dogs of all sorts, for the sofa or the chase; singing birds, poultry, guns, pistols; in short, whatever chance or custom may have rendered saleable. The sellers, excepting in the market of singing birds, which is permanent and large, have no shops, but remain with their wares, either exposed upon the stalls, or hawking them about in their hands. Dogs and birds constitute the principal articles for sale. The pigeon feeders are distinguished in the midst of the mob by long white wands, which they carry to direct the pigeons in their flight. The nobles of Moscow take great delight in these birds: and a favourite pair will sell at from five to ten roubles in the market. I was astonished to see the feeders, by way of exhibiting their birds, let them fly, and recover them again at pleasure. The principal recommendation of the pigeons consists in their rising to a great height, by a spiral curve, all flying one way, and following each other. When a bird is launched, if it does not preserve the line of curvature which the others take, the feeder whistles, waving his wand, and its course is immediately changed. During such exhibitions, the nobles stake their money in wagers, betting upon the height to which a pigeon will ascend, and the number of curves it will make in so doing.

Among dogs for the chase, we observed a noble breed, common in Russia, with long, fine hair, like those of Newfoundland but of amazing size and height, which are used in Russia to hunt wolves. German pug dogs, so dear in London, here bear a low price. I was offered a very fine one for a sum equivalent to an English shilling. We observed, also, English harriers and fox hounds; but the favourite kind of dog, in Moscow, is the English terrier, which is very rare in Russia, and sells for 18 roubles or more, according to the caprice of the buyer and seller. Persian cats were also offered for sale, of a bluish gray, or slate colour, and much admired.

Seeing several stalls apparently covered with wheat, I approached to examine its quality, but was surprised to find that what had the appearance of wheat consisted of large ant's eggs, heaped for sale. Near the same stalls were tubs full of pismires, crawling among the eggs, and over the persons of those who sold them. Both the eggs and the ants are brought to Moscow as food for nightingales, which are favourite, though common birds in Russian houses. They sing, in every respect as beautiful in cages as in their native woods. We often heard them in the bird-shops, warbling with all the fulness and variety of tone which characterizes the nightingale in its natural state. The price of one of them, in full song, is about 15 roubles. The Russians, by rattling beads on their tables of tangible arithmetic, can make the birds sing at pleasure during the day; but nightingales are heard throughout the night, making the streets of the city resound with the melodies of the forest.

Mr. Clarke also observes, that he has been informed that the above method of keeping and feeding of nightingales is becoming prevalent in England.

COLONEL THORNTON.

The family of the Thorntons has been, for some centuries, established in the county of York, where they have enjoyed the most valuable and extensive possessions; and at one period, so large were their domains, that they had the right of sixteen lordships vested in them. The most ancient bears the family name, being still called Thornton cum Bucksby, of which mention is made prior to the period of William the Conqueror.

Sir William Thornton, the grandfather of the present Colonel, was a very active gentleman in supporting the rights and privileges of Englishmen; and such was the estimation in which his talents were held, that he was the individual selected as best calculated to present at the foot of the throne, the articles of the union with Scotland, during the reign of Queen Anne; on which memorable occasion he received the honour of knighthood from her Majesty, accompanied with such demonstrations of royal pleasure as sufficiently indicated that his abilities did not pass unnoticed by his sovereign.

Colonel William Thornton, the father of the subject of these memoirs, bearing all those principles instilled into his mind which had insured his universal approbation, was a ready advocate for the cause of England's rights and liberties, as ratified by the blood of our ancestors.

At the period of the rebellion in Scotland,

this gentleman, anxious to testify his loyalty to his sovereign, raised, at his own expense, a corps of 100 men, whom he fed, clothed, and paid for several months. At the head of this little troop, Colonel William Thornton marched into Scotland, where he joined the main forces under the command of the Duke of Cumberland, and conducted himself at the battles of Falkirk and Culloden with the most intrepid bravery; and such was the publicity of his active conduct that a reward of 1000 pounds was offered by the rebel commanders for his head. After the termination of that eventful struggle, Colonel William Thornton was elected member of Parliament for York.

After a life thus spent in the service of his country, and characterised by every social refinement which adorns human nature, Colonel William Thornton died suddenly, at the age of fifty years, his son being then a minor.

Colonel Thomas Thornton was born in the neighbourhood of St. James's, and placed at a proper age in the Charter-house, in order that he might be near his uncle, who resided in the vicinity of that public seminary.

When fourteen years of age, it was determined that he should go to college, and in consequence he left the Charter-house: the University of Glasgow was preferred, where he was placed by his father, after being introduced to all the leading families residing in that city and its environs.

At this seat of learning our young hero attended to his studies with the most indefatigable assiduity, undergoing the public examinations, in which he acquitted himself to the entire satisfaction of his instructors, and much to his own credit.

Accustomed to pursue the sports of the field during the vacations, which however did not so far infatuate his mind, as to make him relax in his course of studies; in this happy way did he pass his time, until the attainment of his nineteenth year, when he was deprived of the best of fathers. As the death of Colonel William Thornton left the present Colonel sole possessor of his estates, it might be supposed that he instantly quitted Glasgow; such, however, was his good sense, that feeling a conviction how much more remained to be learned, he, on the contrary, still continued for three years at the University, deputing his mother, whom he reverenced with true filial affection, to superintend his affairs.

Previous to this period, the Colonel had imbibed a strong partiality for the pastime of hawking, which he studied with eagerness, being determined to bring that sport to the height of perfection, neither being deterred by expense, nor the difficulties that intervened, to prevent the accomplishment of his darling purpose. At the same period was also laid the foundation of that celebrity, which he has since acquired for his breed of horses and every species of dog calculated for the diversions of the field.

On quitting Glasgow, the Colonel repaired with his hawks, dogs, &c. to his mansion at Old Thornville, where he remained for a few months; after which he visited London, renewed his acquaintance with many of his old college friends, and became a member of the Scavoir Vivre club, which had been very recently instituted.

The leading plan of the Scavoir Vivre was intended to patronize men of genius and talent; whereas it soon became notorious as an institution tolerating every species of licentiousness and debauchery. The late Lord Littleton and the Right Hon. Charles James Fox were then members of that club, as well as many other celebrated characters of the day. It may be necessary to remark, that, although gambling constituted one of the predominent features of the Scavoir Vivre, the Colonel was never led to share that diversion; indeed he was always averse to cards and dice; and to such a pitch did he carry his ideas on that head, that over the chimney-piece of the library of Thornville Royal, is a marble slab whereon are graven the following lines:—

"Utinam hanc veris amicis impleam."

"By the established rule of this house all bets were considered to be off, if either of the parties, by letter, or otherwise, pay into the hands of the landlord one guinea by five the next day."

Having, for a period, followed every diversion which Yorkshire afforded in its fullest extent, Colonel Thornton became desirous of witnessing the sports of the Highlands of Scotland, whither he repaired, accompanied by Mr P. Moseley; and passed the best part of seventeen years in succession, wholly occupied in the several pastimes which were gratifying to his mind.

In order that the pleasures experienced by the Colonel during his continuance to Scotland, might not be confined to his own particular knowledge, he kept a regular diary of the sporting pursuits, &c. and employed an artist to execute drawings of the antiquities and picturesque scenery of the country; from which he afterwards selected a few, and caused them to be engraved in a very finished style, after which he had recourse to his journal: and thus completed a manuscript which, together with the plates, was presented as a donation, to an old school-fellow reduced in his circumstances, and by this means a literary production has been brought into the world under the title of "A Sporting Tour through the Highlands of Scotland, by Colonel Thornton."

At the time of his Majesty's illness, in the year 1789, when debates ran high respecting a regency, very great improvements were carrying on at Allerton Mauleverer, by order of the Duke of York; but on the happy recovery of the King, those plans were almost instantaneously stopped, by the workmen being discharged; and, on the breaking out of the Spanish war, the estate of Allerton was advertised for disposal, when Colonel Thornton determined on purchasing the same, to the no small astonishment of his friends and the neighbouring gentlemen, who did not conceive it possible that he could accomplish such a heavy purchase. However, notwithstanding these conjectures, proposals were made, and at length adjusted; when the Colonel became the purchaser of the estate of Allerton Maulverer, (which he afterwards called Thornville Royal,) for the sum of one hundred and ten thousand pounds, which was paid by instalments, according to the agreement, within twelve months. It is more necessary that this fact should be publicly known, as among other erroneous reports, it has been stated that Colonel Thornton won this estate of the Duke of York at the gaming table.

Soon after this event, the Colonel, being well aware that the wolds were best calculated for the purpose of coursing and hawking, purchased of Mr. Bilby the estate of Boythorp, on the wolds, for the sum of ten thousand pounds, where he erected the present mansion, known by the name of Falconer's Hall.

During the sporting career of Colonel Thornton, his mansion of Thornville was always the scene of festive hospitality; and it may with truth be said, that no gentleman is better calculated to preside at the board of hilarity. His diversified talents, his quickness of repartee, his facetious stories on all topics, and his good-natured acquiescence with the request of his guests, have ever rendered his table the resort of the neighbouring noblemen and gentlemen. Nor ought we to pass unnoticed the excellence and abundance of his wines, which were always of the first quality.

With respect to the works of art which adorned the mansion-house of Thornville, few dwellings had to boast a more diversified and choice collection of paintings; and, with respect to sporting subjects, it is only necessary to remark, that the most celebrated pictures of Gilpin and Reinagle, painted under the immediate direction of the Colonel, were there to be found. The well-known picture of the Death of the Fox, by Gilpin, an unrivalled performance; which has since been engraved by Scott, in his best manner, affording a great treat, not only to the sporting world, but to all admirers of fine engraving.—Among other masters of the Italian and Flemish schools, which characterized the Thornville collection, were Guido, Carracci, Teniers, Wouwerman, Rubens, Vandyke, &c. &c.

With respect to the sporting animals reared by Colonel Thornton, it will be merely requisite to instance a few, which, from their acknowledged excellence, sufficiently prove the judgment of the Colonel in every point relating to the breed of animals connected with field-sports.

HORSES.—Icelander. A noted racer, bred by Colonel Thornton, which won twenty-six matches, and was the first foal bred by the Colonel. The sire of this horse was Grey-coat, and his grandsire Dismal.

Jupiter.—This celebrated blood-horse was of a chestnut colour, he was got by Eclipse, dam by Tartar, grandam by Mogul, Sweepstakes, &c. in 1777, he won one thousand pounds at Lewes; two hundred at Abington; and one thousand at Newmarket: and, in 1771, two hundred and forty at Newmarket.

Truth—A remarkable steady hunter.

Stoic—A famous race-horse, which won a match at Newmarket for one thousand guineas.

St. Thomas—A race-horse, which beat Mr. Hare's Tu Quoque, the bet being five hundred guineas, each gentleman riding his own horse.

Thornville—A celebrated hunter.

Esterhazy—A most remarkable blood-horse, being master of any weight, and active in all his paces; of which animal a very beautiful engraving has been executed by Ward, from a picture of Chalon.

DOGS.—Fox-hounds.—Merlin—A well known fox-hound, bred by Colonel Thornton.

Lucifer—A most remarkable fox-hound, the sire of Lounger and Mad Cap, of equal celebrity.

Old Conqueror—A matchless fox-hound, sire

of many well-known dogs in the annals of fox-hunting.

POINTERS.—Dash—An acknowledged fine pointer, which sold for two hundred and fifty guineas.

Pluto—A celebrated pointer.

Juno—A remarkable bitch, which was matched with a pointer of Lord Grantley's for ten thousand guineas, who paid forfeit.

Modish—A bitch of acknowledged excellence.

Lily—A most remarkable steady bitch.

Nan—It is only necessary to state that seventy-five guineas were refused for this bitch.

GREYHOUNDS.—Major—A dog of very great celebrity, and the father of Colonel Thornton's present breed of greyhounds. Of this animal a very beautiful engraving, from the masterly hand of Scott, has been published.

Czarina—A bitch of equal celebrity.

Skyagraphina—A matchless hound. N. B. For each of these hounds the most extravagant sums have been offered, but rejected.

SPANIELS.—Dash—This animal is esteemed the ne plus ultra of this species of sporting dog; the Colonel having used his utmost endeavours to bring the spaniel to perfection.

BEAGLES.—Merryman—This celebrated dog is sire to a pack, which exceeds all others for symmetry, bottom, and pace. The beagles of

Colonel Thornton will tire the strongest hunters, and return to kennel comparatively fresh.

TERRIERS.—It would be necessary to notice Colonel Thornton's Terriers, if it were only on account of his justly celebrated Pitch, from whom are descended most of the white terriers in this kingdom.

HAWKS.—Sans Quartier, Death, and the Devil, were three of the most celebrated birds ever reared by Colonel Thornton during his pursuit of hawking, and were allowed to distance any birds of the kind which ever had been flown at the game.

In speaking of the bodily activity of Colonel Thornton, few men perhaps have ever given proofs of such extraordinary powers. Among various other matches of a similar nature, the following, it is conceived, will be amply sufficient to substantiate this fact:—

In a walking match, which the Colonel engaged to perform, he went four miles in thirty-two minutes and half a second.

In leaping, Colonel Thornton cleared his own height, being five feet nine inches, the bet being considerable.

In another match it is stated, that he leaped over six five-barred gates in six minutes, and then repeated the same on horseback.

At Newmarket the Colonel, on horseback, ran down a hare, which he picked up, in the presence of an immense concourse of people assembled to witness this extraordinary match.

With respect to shooting, either with the fowling-piece, rifle, or air-gun, Colonel Thornton has given the most incontestible proofs of the steadiness of his hand and the wonderful correctness of his sight, not only in bringing down the game, when pursuing the pastimes of the field, but also at a mark, in which his precision has never been surpassed.

Notwithstanding the numerous pursuits of a sporting nature, which occupied the Colonel's mind, he has seldom lost sight of those refinements which characterize the man of literature and taste. His valuable collection of pictures, at his last seat of Thornville Royal, sufficiently indicate his taste for the fine arts, and the correct journals which he invariably kept during all his excursions to Scotland, &c. as well as the artists who always attended him to take drawings of the scenery characteristic of the country through which he passed, are sufficient testimonies of his diversified talents and classic pursuits.

During the short interval of peace which occurred between this country and France, in 1802, the Colonel repaired to Paris, for the purpose of viewing that capital; after which, he travelled through the southern provinces, and part of the conquered territory, where her pursued, with avidity, the sports which characterize that kingdom. On this occasion the Colonel had an artist to accompany him, while, as in every other instance, he kept a journal of the events that transpired. From this diary, a very entertaining tour has been produced, intituled, "Colonel Thornton's Sporting Tour through France," &c. which from the variety and excellence of the picturesque illustrations with which it abounds, very justly takes precedence of almost every work of a similar description already before the public. In the course of this Tour appears a very entertaining and curious comparative view of the sports of the two countries, which the Colonel's acknowledged excellence as an English sportsman, has rendered not only entertaining, but scientific and useful. These materials form the subject of upwards of forty letters, which were afterwards sent to his noble friend the Earl of Darlington, to whom this splendid work is dedicated.

This gentleman is not only devoted to the pursuits of Actæon and the pleasures of Bacchus, but Venus and Cupid are likewise his idols, having, in the autumn of 1806, led to the hymenial altar Miss Corston, of Essex, an accomplished young lady, of some fortune.

Upon the Colonel's giving up his commission as Lieutenant-colonel of the West York militia, he was drawn into York by the soldiery, who, as a testimony of their gratitude and love, presented him with a beautiful medallion and splendid sword, which the Colonel to the present hour esteems as the most precious badge of honour that could be bestowed.

With respect to the corporeal pains incidental to human nature, Colonel Thornton to all appearance is perfectly unacquainted with them: he has experienced the most trying accidents, but the hand of fate seems always to have been extended to preserve him. Rest is generally esteemed the balm of human life; yet the Col. has copiously drank of the juice of the grape and remained with his friends till the return of dawn; he still is awake at the usual hour, and, while the world is buried in sleep, he frequently occupies an hour or two free from headache, with a mind calm and collected.

It is evident the Colonel has imbibed one opinion, viz.—" Time is precious: life is but a span; we should therefore make the best use of it." In fine, the greatest persecution that could be entailed on Colonel Thornton would be to condemn him to pass a week in idleness: his mind, ever on the alert, pictures some new scene for action; and, if the object be but trivial, we had better occupy the mind on that nothingness, than suffer the fancy to lie dormant, and fix on things derogatory to our natures.

The fine collection of Sporting Paintings, belonging to Colonel Thornton, were sold by auction at Hickeman's Gallery, St. James's Street, June, 1819.

SPORTING INTREPIDITY DISPLAYED BY MRS. THORNTON.

The lady of Colonel Thornton, it seems, is equally attached to the sports of the field, with her distinguished husband; and the singular contest which took place between Mrs. Thornton and Mr. Flint, in 1804, not only stands recorded on the annals of the turf, as one of the most remarkable occurrences which ever happened in the sporting world, but likewise a lasting monument of female intrepidity. The following are the circumstances which gave rise to this extraordinary race.

An intimacy once existed between the families of Colonel Thornton and Mr. Flint, the two ladies being sisters, when the latter gentleman frequently partook of the exilarating bottle at the hospitable board of Thornville Royal.

In the course of one of their equestrian excursions in Thornville Park, the lady of Col. Thornton and Mr. Flint were conversing on the qualities of their respective horses; and (as it generally happens where a spirit of rivalry exists) the difference of opinion was great, and the horses were occasionally put at full speed for the purpose of ascertaining the point in question; Old Vingarillo, aided by the skilfulness of his fair rider, distanced his antagonist every time, which so discomfited Mr. Flint, that he was at length induced to challenge the lady to ride on a future day. This challenge was readily accepted (on the part of the lady) by Colonel Thornton; and it was agreed that the race should take place on the last day of the York August meeting, 1804. This curious match was announced in the following manner :—

"A match for 500gs. and 1000gs. bye—four miles—between Colonel Thornton's Vingarillo, and Mr. Flint's br. h. Thornville, by Volunteer.—Mrs. Thornton to ride her weight against Mr. Flint's."

On Saturday, August 25, this race took place, the following description of which appeared in the York Herald :—

"Never did we witness such an assemblage of people as were drawn together on the above occasion—100,000 at least. Nearly ten times the number appeared on Knavesmire that did on the day when Bay Malton ran, or when Eclipse went over the course, leaving the two best horses of the day a mile and a half behind. Indeed expectation was raised to the highest pitch, from the novelty of the match. Thousands from every part of the surrounding country thronged to the ground. In order to keep the course as clear as possible, several additional people were employed; and, much to the credit of the 6th Light Dragoons, a party of them also were on the ground on horseback, for the like purpose, and which unquestionably was the cause of many lives being saved.

"About four o'clock, Mrs. Thornton appeared on the ground, full of spirit, her horse led by Colonel Thornton, and followed by Mr. Baker, and Mr. H. Boynton; afterwards appeared Mr. Flint. They started a little past four o'clock. The lady took the lead for upwards of three miles, in a most capital style. Her horse, however, had much the shorter stroke of the two. When within a mile of being home, Mr. Flint pushed forward, and got the lead, which he kept. Mrs. Thornton used every exertion; but finding it impossible to win the race, she drew up, in a sportsmanlike style when within about two distances.

"At the commencement of the running, the bets were 5 and 6 to 4 on the lady: in running the three first miles, 7 to 4 and 2 to 1 in her favour. Indeed the oldest sportsmen on the stand thought she must have won. In running the last mile, the odds were in favour of Mr. Flint.

"Never surely did a woman ride in a better style. It was difficult to say whether her horsemanship, her dress, or her beauty, were most admired—the tout ensemble was unique.

"Mrs. Thornton's dress was a leopard-coloured body, with blue sleeves, the rest buff, and blue cap. Mr. Flint rode in white. The race was run in nine minutes and fifty-nine seconds.

"Thus ended the most interesting races ever ran upon Knavesmire. No words can express the disappointment felt at the defeat of Mrs. Thornton. The spirit she displayed, and the good humour with which she has borne her loss, have greatly diminished the joy of many of the winners. From the very superior style in which she performed her exercising gallop of four miles on Wednesday, betting was greatly in her favour; for the accident which happened, in consequence of her saddle-girths having slackened, and the saddle turning round, was not attended with the slightest injury to her person, nor did it in the least damp her courage; while her horsemanship, and close seated riding, astonished the beholders, and inspired a general confidence in her success.

" Not less than 200,000l. were pending upon Mrs. Thornton's match; perhaps more, if we include the bets in every part of the country, and there is no part, we believe, in which there were not some.

" It will be seen, by the time of performance, that Haphazard was the best horse at the meeting. Seldom have we witnessed a meeting at York, where the races have been so well contested. Almost the whole have been run, and the horses rode in a style of great superiority. To add to the pleasure attending the meeting, the weather has been most favourable, and the company numerous and fashionable."

It is but justice to observe, that if the lady had been better mounted, she could not possibly have failed of success. Indeed she laboured under every possible disadvantage; notwithstanding which, and the ungallant conduct of Mr. Flint; she flew along the course with an astonishing swiftness, conscious of her own superior skill, and would ultimately, have outstripped her adversary, but for the accident which took place.

FEROCITY OF THE LYNX.

From the "Moniteur."

They write from Notre Dame de la Rose, that four ferocious animals, commonly called Lynxes (loups cerviers) had been in the arrondizement, in November, 1817, having cleared the forests of Collobrieres. On receiving the first account of their appearance, the farmers armed themselves and went in pursuit. The alarm spread from commune to commune, and speedily there was a general battue. They were soon dispersed, and three of them were killed successively. One of them, about the size of a large dog, passed through a flock without doing any harm, and ran at the shepherd, who owed his safety to his two dogs. In another quarter, he attacked an unfortunate woman, whom he bit severely, and whose life was despaired of. At length, he sought refuge in the territory of the commune of Pignans, where he found his conqueror in a peasant of extraordinary strength, made like a Hercules, and in the bloom of life. This man, who was unarmed, seized him body to body, and after a sanguinary and obstinate struggle, which lasted three quarters of an hour, succeeded in throwing him to the ground; but still he would not have conquered him but for his address and promptitude. This furious animal had devoured the hat of his adversary; a large buckle attached to the hat, stuck between his teeth; the man availed himself of this circumstance, and having courageously thrust his hand, armed with a stone, into his mouth, as deep as possible, left the stone there, and in spite of the numerous bites which he received, did not let go his hold until he tore out the tongue of the animal, flung him to the ground, and saw him expire in dreadful convulsions. This trait of rare intrepidity has excited the admiration of the whole country.

THE ARCHER'S SONG.

Bright Phœbus! thou patron of poets below,
   Assist me of Archers to sing;
For you we esteem as the god of the Bow,
   As well as the god of the String,
                       My old Buck!

The fashion of shooting 'twas you who began,
   When you shot forth your beams from the skies,
The sly urchin Cupid first follow'd the plan,
   And the goddesses shot with their eyes,
                       The bright Girls!

DIANA, who slaughtered the brutes with her darts,
   Shot only one lover or so;

For VENUS excell'd her in shooting at hearts,
  And had always more strings to her bow,
          A sly Jade!

On beautiful IRIS, Apollo bestow'd
  A bow of most wonderful hue;
It soon grew her hobby-horse, and as she rode
  On it, like an arrow she flew,
          Gaudy Dame!

To earth came the art of the Archers at last,
  And were follow'd with eager pursuit;
But the sons of APOLLO all others surpass,
  With such very long *bows* do they shoot,
          Lying Dogs!

ULYSSES, the hero of Greece, long ago
  In courage and strength did excel;
So he left in his house an inflexible *bow*,
  And a far more inflexible *belle*,
          Lucky Rogue!

The Parthians were bowmen of old, and their pride
  Lay in shooting, and scampering too;
But Britons thought better the sport to divide,
  So they *shot*, and their enemies *flew*,
          The Brave Boys!

Then a health to the brave British bowmen be crown'd;
  May their courage ne'er sit in the dark;
May their strings be all good, and their bows be all sound,
  And their arrows fly true to the mark,
          British Boys!

RUSSIAN PUGILISM.

Though the Russian boor is far more hardy than the English peasant, yet one of the latter would conquer half a dozen Russians in the battle of the fist. A tourist in the north of Europe gives the following anecdote upon this subject, at St. Petersburgh:—" As I was quitting the place, two fellows, somewhat tipsy, began to quarrel, and, after abusing each other very violently as they walked along, they at last proceeded to blows. No pugilistic science was displayed; they fought with their hands extended as awkwardly as women playing at battledore and shuttlecock. A police-officer soon appeared, and taking a cord from his pocket, tied the combattants back to back, and placing them upon a droska, galloped off to the nearest siega."

AN ENORMOUS BOAR KILLED IN THE FOREST OF WALLINCOURT, BY THE DUKE OF WELLINGTON.

CAMBRAY, Oct. 30, 1817.—The hounds of the Duke of Wellington, discovered a most enormous boar, in the forest of Wallincourt. The animal, on being disturbed, passed rapidly into the forest of Ardipart, which he completely traversed; being then hardly scented by the dogs, he took the plain, where he was vigourously pursued by hounds and sportsmen, and ere he could reach another road was brought to bay. The animal then became ferocious, and destroyed all the dogs that approached him, when one of his Grace's aides-du-camp plunged his spear into his side. This only rendered the beast more savage, when his Grace himself, seeing his dogs would be destroyed, rode up, and with his spear gave the coup de grace; the animal made a desperate effort to wound his

Grace's horse, and fell in the attempt. The peasants say he is the largest boar that has been seen for some years. Of the numerous field that started in the pursuit, only five, besides his Grace, reached the end.

THE OLD SHEPHERD'S DOG.

BY PETER PINDAR.

The old Shepherd's Dog, like his master was gray,
  His teeth all departed and feeble his tongue;
Yet where'er *Corin* went, he was follow'd by *Tray*,—
  Thus happy through life did they hobble along.

When fatigued, on the grass the Shepherd would lie,
  For a nap in the sun—'midst his slumbers so sweet,
His faithful companion crawl'd constantly nigh,
  Plac'd his head on his lap, or lay down at his feet.

When winter was heard on the hill and the plain,
  And torrents descended, and cold was the wind;
If *Corin* went forth 'mid the tempest and rain,
  Tray scorn'd to be left in the chimney behind.

At length in the straw *Tray* made his last bed:
  For vain, against Death, is the stoutest endeavour;
To lick *Corin's* hand he rear'd up his weak head;
  Then fell back, clos'd his eyes, and ah! clos'd them for ever.

Not long after *Tray* did the Shepherd remain,
  Who oft o'er his grave with true sorrow would bend,
And, when dying, thus feebly was heard the poor swain,
  "O, bury me, neighbours, beside my old Friend."

SAGACITY OF BEES.

A swarm of Bees, which had just hived, went into a fruit shop on the North Bridge, Edinburgh. They had been attracted in their flight by the smell of honey, and the fruit in the shop. This affords a striking proof of the uncommon acuteness and sensibility of these wonderful insects.— They continued in the shop and on the windows for several hours, to the great entertainment of the spectators, till a person acquainted with the management of bees, got hold of the Queen Bee, and induced them to go into a hive.

SINGULAR OCCURRENCE.—A BIRD CAUGHT BY A FISH.

In a pond near Lewes, in Sussex, a pike, in appearance about a foot long, was seen to seize and gradually gorge a swallow, (probably one of the webb-footed kind,) as it was wantoning on the surface of the water. The above is an indubitable fact, as witnessed and related by a clergyman, whose veracity cannot be disputed, and on whose authority we feel a pleasure in recording this piscatory anecdote.

THE HONEY GUIDE.

While travelling in the interior of Africa, Mr. Parke had frequent opportunities of observing the conduct of that remarkable bird, called the Honey Guide, mentioned by Dr. Sparman, and other naturalists who have travelled into Africa. It is a curious species of the Wokow, and derives its name from its singular quality of discovering wild honey to travellers. Honey is the favourite food of this bird: and morning and evening being the time of feeding, it is then heard calling in a shrill tone, cherr, cherr, which the honey-hunters carefully attend to as the summons to the chase. At last the bird is observed to hover for a few minutes over a certain spot, and then silently retiring to a neighbouring bush, or other resting-place, the hunters are sure of finding the bees' nest in that identical spot, whether it be in a tree, or in the crevice of a rock. The bee-hunters never fail to leave a small portion for their conductor, but commonly take care not to leave so much as would satisfy his hunger. The bird's appetite being only whetted by this parsimony, it is obliged to commit a second treason, by discovering another bees' nest, in hopes of a better salary. It is further observed, that the nearer the bird approaches to the hidden hive, the more frequently it repeats its call, and seems the more impatient.

WASPS.

The injury they do the fruit, and the offensive nature of the insect, make it a desirable object for naturalists to turn their attention to the best means of destroying them. It is a curious fact in the natural history of this insect, that the males are almost all destroyed by one another, or perish with cold in the severity of the weather, and that some few of the females only survive to lay their eggs, and hatch new swarms in the succeeding summer.—From this peculiarity it is said, that every single wasp destroyed between the months of January and May saves a nest, for a single female wasp will generate 10,000 before the end of August. Should it not then be a general object to destroy them during the early months of the year: and what would be the best means of hunting them out?

SPANISH BULL-BAITING.

The Bull fights at Madrid, generally commence in April, and attract immense multitudes in the arena constructed for that purpose. The inclination of the people for the sanguinary part of this spectacle may be judged of from the receipts of the morning and afternoon performance, as under mentioned.

In the morning only six bulls were to be run, and the produce of the seats amounted altogether to 45,950 rials. In the afternoon, when ten bulls were slaughtered, the money taken was 72,019 rials. Nineteen horses were killed during the attacks, by the impetuous goadings of the maddened animals, the skin of which, with that of the sixteen bulls, and a contribution of the people admitted to sell water to the spectators, amounted altogether to 126,528 rials for the day's exertion; in justification of which humanity seems to exclaim, that no other argument can possibly be adduced than that the profit is applied to the support of the hospitals of Madrid.

CURIOUS WAGER.—WALKING AGAINST EATING.

This sporting event was decided at a public house at Knightsbridge: one Boyne, a labouring gardener undertook for the trifling sum of half a crown to eat, without drinking, 24 red herrings, and two ounces of mustard, while the landlord, a corpulent man, walked half a mile on the road. The pedestrian performed his march in somewhat less than nine minutes; but the hero of the jaw-bone had in less than eight minutes completed his task, and waited the arrival of his opponent with a full pot, the first fruits of his victory.

SINGULAR CRICKET MATCHES AND RACES BETWEEN ELEVEN MEN WITH ONE LEG AGAINST THE SAME NUMBER WITH ONE ARM, ALL OF THE MEN GREENWICH PENSIONERS.

From the novelty of an advertisement announcing a Cricket-Match to be played by eleven Greenwich Pensioners with one leg against eleven with one arm, for one thousand guineas, at the new Cricket-Ground, Montpelier-Gardens, Walworth, in 1796, an immense concourse of people assembled. About nine o'clock the men arrived in three Greenwich stages; about ten the wickets were pitched, and the match commenced. Those with but one leg had the first innings, and got ninety-three runs. About three o'clock, while those with but one arm were having their innings, a scene of riot and confusion took place, owing to the pressure of the populace to gain admittance to the ground: the gates were forced open, and several parts of the fencing were broken down, and a great number of persons having got upon the roof of a stable, the roof broke in, and several persons falling among the horses were taken out much bruised. About six o'clock the game was renewed, and those with one arm got but forty-two runs during their innings. The one legs commenced their second innings, and six 'were bowled out, after they got sixty runs, so that they left off one hundred and eleven more than those with one arm.

The match was played again on the Wednesday following, and the men with one leg beat the one arms by one hundred and three runnings.

After the match was finished, the eleven one-legged men ran one hundred yards for twenty guineas. The three first divided the money.

AN EXTRAORDINARY SHOT.

A Clergyman, in the eastern part of Sussex, a few years since, at a single discharge of his gun, killed a partridge, shot a man, a hog, and a hogsty, broke fourteen panes of glass, and knocked down six gingerbread kings and queens that were standing on the mantle-piece opposite the window. The above may be depended upon as a fact, not exaggerated, but given literally as it happened.

THE LATE RIGHT HONOURABLE MR. FOX, AS A SPORTING CHARACTER.

This distinguished personage was at the head of every thing in which he was engaged. He ranked with the best players, and excelled most at Whist, Quintz, and all the fashionable games of skill. But Horse-racing was his darling amusement, till he quitted the turf, and all other play, from prudential motives. He played at other games with indifference. He would throw for a thousand guineas with as much sang-froid, as when he has played at Tetotum for a shilling. But when his horse ran he was all eagerness and anxiety. He always placed himself where the horse was to make the push or where the race was to be most strongly contested. From thence he eyed the horses advancing with the most immovable look, he breathed quicker as they accelerated their pace, and when they came opposite him, he rode in with them on full speed, whipping, spurring, and blowing, as if he would have infused his whole soul in the courage, speed, and perseverance of his favourite racer. But the race being over, whether he won or lost it seemed to make no impression upon him, and he immediately directed his conversation to the next race, whether he had a horse to run or not.

AN INGENIOUS MORALITY ON CHESS.
By Pope Innocent.

This world is nearly like a chess-board, one point of which is white, the other black, because of the double state of life and death, grace and sin. The families of this chess-board are like the men of this world: they all come out of one bag, and are placed in different stations in this world, and have different appellations, one is called King, another Queen, the third Rook, the fourth Knight, the fifth Alphin, the sixth Pawn.

The condition of the game is, that one takes another; and when the game is finished, as they all come out of one bag, they are put in the same place together. Neither is there any difference between the king and the poor pawn; and it often happens, that when thrown promiscuously into the bag, the king lies at the bottom; just as the great will find themselves in their transit from this world to hell. In this game the King goes and takes in all the circumjacent places in a direct line: a sign the king takes every thing justly, and that he never must omit doing justice to all uprightly; for in whatever manner a king acts, it is reputed just; and what pleases the sovereign has the vigour of law.

The Queen, whom we call Fen, goes and takes in an oblique line: because women, being an avaricious breed (genus,) whatever they take beyond their merit and grace, is rapine and injusticce.

The Rook is a judge, who perambulates the whole land in a straight line, and should not take any thing in an oblique manner by bribery and corruption, nor spare any one. Thus they verify the saying of Amos—" Ye have turned judgment into gall, and the fruits of righteousness into hemlock !"

But the Knight, in taking, goes one point directly, and then takes an oblique circuit; a sign that knights and lords of the land may justly take the rents due to them, and their just fines, from those who have forfeited them, according to the exigence of the case; their third part being obliquely, applies to them, so far as they extort subsidies and unjust exactions from their subjects.

The poor Pawn goes directly forward, in his simplicity; but whenever he will take, does so obliquely. Thus man, while he rests satisfied with his poverty, lives in a direct line; but when he craves temporal honours, by means of lies perjuries, favours, and adulation, he goes obliquely, till he reaches the superior degree of the chess board of this world; then the pawn changes to fen, and is elevated to the rank of the point he reaches, just like poverty promoted to rank, fortune, and consequently insolence.

The Alphins are the various prelates of the church, pope, archbishop, and their subordinate bishops, who rise to their sees not so much by divine inspiration, as by royal power, interest, entreaties, and ready money. These Alphins move and take obliquely three points; for almost every prelate's mind is perverted by love, hatred, or bribery; not to reprehend the guilty, or bark against the vicious, but rather to absolve them of their sins: so that those who should have extirpated vice, are, in consequence of their parsimony, become promoters of vice, and advocates of the devil.

In this chess-game the devil says " Check !" whenever he insults and strikes one with his dart of sin; and, if he that is struck cannot immediately deliver himself, the devil, resuming the move, says to him, " Mate !" carrying his soul along with him to prison, from which neither love nor money can redeem him—for from hell there is no redemption. And as huntsmen have various hounds for taking various beasts, so the devil and the world have different vices, which differently entangle mankind—for all that is in the world, is either lust of the flesh, lust of the eyes, or proud living.

YORKSHIRE FIGHTING.
From Mr. RYLEY's "*Itinerant.*"

At length the company were summoned into the barn, to witness a battle between two noted Yorkshire fighters. Amidst the crowd I perceived two men naked to their waists lying on the ground, grappling each other, perfectly silent, and sometimes pretty still; then, as if moved by one impulse, a desperate scuffle took place; soon, however, the one extricated himself, quickly obtained his legs, and retreating some paces, returned with great violence, and before his antagonist could rise, kicked in three of his ribs: the vanquished lay prostrate, whilst the victor stamped and roared like a madman, challenging all around. Retiring to my seat in the house, disgusted with Yorkshire Fighting, I determined to finish my wine, and leave the brutes to the enjoyment of their brutality, when a laughable circumstance detained me, and in some measure made amends for the misery I had suffered.—There is, I believe, a respectable personage, who amongst amateurs in sporting, bears the appellation of a Belward, a gentleman who gets his livelihood by leading a bear by the nose from village to village; such an one now arrived at this public house, and placing his companion in the pigsty, seated himself by the fire, and called for a pint of ale. The Yorkshire warrior, elated with his victory, and intoxicated with liquor, went from room to room, and bade defiance to every one; on entering the kitchen, he espied the Belward, who, being a stout fellow, and a noted pugilist, was immediately requested to take a turn with him—"No, no," replied the stranger, "I don't like Yorkshire fighting; hugging, biting, and kicking, does not suit me; but

I have a friend without who is used to them there things: if you like, I'll fetch him in?" "Ay, ay, dom him, fot him in: I'll fight ony mon i' th' country." The Belward repaired to the pigsty, and brought forth Bruin, who from a large sized quadruped, was changed instantly to a most tremendous biped. In this erect posture he entered the house, and as it was nearly dark, the intoxicated countryman was the more easily imposed upon—"Dom thee," he said, "I'll fight a better mon than thee, either up or down," and made an attempt to seize him round the middle, but feeling the roughness of his hide, he exclaimed—"Come, come, I'll tak no advantage; poo off thy top coat, and I'll fight thee for a crown."

The bear not regarding this request, gave him such a hug as 'tis probable he never before experienced; it nearly pressed the breath out of his body, and proved, what was before doubted, that there was as great a bear in the village as himself.

THE HUMBLE PETITION OF DUCE,

AN OLD POINTER.

Pity the sorrows of a poor old dog,
Whose trembling limbs your helping hand require;
Permit her still to crawl about your house,
Or rest contented near your kitchen fire.

Oft' for your sport I brush'd the morning dew,
Oft' rang'd the stubble where the partridge lay;
Well pleas'd I labour'd;—for I toil'd for you,
Nor wish for respite till the setting day.

With you, my good old master, I have rov'd,
Or up the hill or down the murm'ring brook;
When game was near, no joint about me mov'd,
I strove to guess your wishes by your look.

While you with busy care prepar'd the gun,
I frisk'd and sported by my master's side,
Obey'd with ready eye your sign to run,
Yet still abhor'd the thoughts of ranging wide.

O these were days be they remember'd still,
Pleas'd I review the moments that are past;
I never hurt the gander by the mill,
Nor saw the miller's wife stand all aghast.

I never slunk from the good farmer's yard;
The tender chicken liv'd secure for me;
Though hunger prest, I never thought it hard,
Nor left you whistling underneath the tree.

Those days, alas! no longer smile on me;
No more I snuff the morning's scented gale,
No more I hear the gun with wonted glee,
Or scour with rapture thro' the sedgy vale.

For now old age relaxes all my frame,
Unnerves my limbs, and dims my feeble eyes;
Forbids my once swift feet the road to fame,
And the fond crust, alas! untasted lies!

Then take me to your hospitable fire,
There let me dream of thousand coveys slain;
There rest, till all the pow'rs of nature tire,
Nor dread an age of misery and pain.

Let me with Driver,* my old faithful friend;
Upon his bed of straw sigh out my days;
So blessings on your head shall still descend,
And, well as pointer can, I'll sing your praise.

Pity the sorrows of your poor old Duce,
Whose trembling limbs your helping hand require;
Permit him still to crawl about your house,
Or rest contented near your kitchen fire.

* A favourite horse.

THE IVORY-BILLED WOODPECKER OF NORTH AMERICA.

From Mr. Wilson's "American Ornithology."

This majestic and formidable species, in strength and magnitude, stands at the head of the whole class of Woodpeckers hitherto discovered. He may be called the king or chief of his tribe; and nature seems to have designed him a distinguished characteristic in the superb carmine crest, and bill of polished ivory, with which she has ornamented him. His eye is brilliant and daring, and his whole frame so admirably adapted to his mode of life, and method of procuring subsistence, as to impress on the mind of the examiner the most reverential ideas of the Creator. His manners have also a dignity in them superior to the common herd of Woodpeckers. Trees, shrubbery, orchards, rails, fence posts, and old prostrate logs, are alike interesting to those, in their humble and indefatigable search for prey; but the royal hunter now before us, scorns the humility of such situations, and seeks the most towering trees of the forest, seeming particularly attached to those prodigious cypress swamps, whose crowded giant sons stretch their bare and blasted or moss-hung arms midway to the skies. In their almost inaccessible recesses, amidst ruinous piles of impending timber, his trumpet-like note and loud strokes resound through the solitary savage wilds, of which he seems the sole lord and inhabitant. Wherever he frequents, he leaves numerous monuments of his industry behind him. We there see enormous pine trees, with cart-loads of bark lying round their roots, and chips of the trunk itself, in such quantities, as to suggest the idea that half a dozen of axe-men had been at work there for the whole morning. The body of the tree is also disfigured with such numerous and so large excavations, that one can hardly conceive it possible for the whole to be the work of a Woodpecker. With such strength, and an apparatus so powerful, what havoc might he not commit, if numerous, on the most useful of our forest trees; and yet, with all these apppearances, and much of vulgar prejudice against him, it may fairly be questioned whether he is at all injurious, or, at least, whether his exertions do not contribute most powerfully to the protection of our timber. Examine closely the tree where he has been at work, and you will soon perceive that it is neither from motives of mischief or amusement that he slices off the brrk, or digs his way into the trunk—for the sound and healthy tree is not the object of his attention. The diseased, infested with insects, and hastening to putrefaction, are his favourites; there the deadly crawling enemy have formed a lodgment, between the bark and tender wood, to drink up the vital part of the tree. It is the ravages of these vermin which the intelligent proprietor of the forest deplores as the sole perpetrators of the destruction of his timber. Would it be believed that the larvæ of an insect, or fly, no larger than a grain of rice should silently, and in one season, destroy some thousand acres of pine trees, many of them from two to three feet in diameter, and a hundred and fifty feet high! Yet, whoever passes along the high road from Georgetown and Charlestown, in South Carolina, about twenty miles from the former place, can have striking and melancholy proofs of this fact. In some places, the whole woods, as far as you can see around you, are dead, stripped of their bark, their wintry-looking arms are bare trunks bleaching in the sun, and tumbling in ruins before every blast, presenting a frightful picture of desolation.

In looking over the accounts given of the ivory-billed Woodpecker by the naturalists of Europe, I find it asserted, that it inhabits from New-Jersey to Mexico. I believe, however, that few of them are ever seen to the north of Virginia, and very few of them even in that state. The first place I observed this bird at, when on my way to the south, was about 12 miles north of Wilmington, in North Carolina. There I found the bird, from which the drawing of the figure in the plate was taken. This bird was only wounded slightly in the wing; and on being caught, uttered a loudly reiterated and most piteous note, exactly resembling the violent crying of a young child, which terrified my horse, so as nearly to have cost me my life. It was distressing to hear it. I carried it with me in the chair, under cover to Wilmington. In passing through the streets, its affecting cries surprised every one within hearing, particularly the females, who hurried to the doors and windows with looks of alarm and anxiety. I drove on; and on arriving at the piazza of the hotel, where I intended to put up, the landlord came forward, and a number of other persons who happened to be there, all equally alarmed at what they heard; this was greatly increased by my asking, whether he could furnish me with accommodations for myself and baby.—The man looked blank and foolish, while the others stared with still greater astonishment. After diverting myself for a minute or two at their expense, I drew my Woodpecker from under the cover, and a general laugh took place. I took him up stairs, and locked him up in my room, while I went to see my horse taken care of. In less than an hour I returned, and on opening the door he set up the same distressing shout, which now appeared to proceed from grief, that he had been discovered in his attempt to escape. He had mounted along the side of the window, nearly as high as the ceiling, a little below which he had begun to break through. The bed was covered with large pieces of plaster; the lath was exposed for at least 15 inches square, and a hole large enough to admit the fist, opened to the weather-boards, so that in less than another hour, he would certainly have succeeded in making his way through. I now tied a string round his leg, and fastened it to the table, and again left him. I wished to preserve his life, and had gone off in search of suitable food for him. As I re-ascended the stairs, I heard him again hard at work; and on entering, had the mortification of perceiving that he had almost entirely ruined the mahogany table to which he was fastened, and on which he had wreaked his whole vengeance. While engaged in taking the drawing, he cut me in several places: and, on the whole, displayed such a noble and unconquerable spirit, that I was frequently tempted to restore him to his native woods. He lived with me nearly three days, but refused all sustenance; and I witnessed his death with regret.

THE CHASE—A SHANDEAN FRAGMENT.

By this time the hunters had disappeared, and in about twenty minutes a labourer came out of the cottage, and informed us that the stag was coming down the hill in full view, and that we should see the chase to the best advantage from the back door of the house.

The buck, to which the huntsman had given but short law, came bounding down a slope, pursued by the hounds in full cry, the hunters, close in with the dogs, hallooing, "tantivy, tantivy," at every stretch.

"This is a view hollow," said I, turning to Captain O'Carrol.

The poor animal had made a circuit, to gain the place where he was first raised, but finding neither safety nor covert there, he turned round, ran right ahead, and in so doing crossed the garden of the cottage where we stood.

Two dogs and men passed on.

Two ladies rode by, pushing their horses with a degree of courage and vigour that would do honour to the spirit and strength of Amazons.

A third female, fearless as Camilla, closed the chase; it was Heaven's mercy she did not close her life. Unhappy fair one! with whip and spur she urged the courser's speed; but just as she prepared to clear a fence, the bank gave way, and down came the horse, jirking the rider from its back into the middle of the ditch.

We ran to her assistance; she was topsy turvy.

"This is a view hollow," said O'Carrol, turning to me.

Sophia retired a few paces.

"We must fix her upon her feet," said O'Carrol, leaping into the ditch, and seizing the lady by the binding of her petticoats; I followed his example.

An old virtuoso came up, he took out his

glass,—"I believe she is a peeress," said he, by the coronet on her saddle."

'Twas not possible to turn the lady, either on one side or the other.

A labourer came to our assistance; he got under the lady, and raised her.

"Bless my eyes," exclaimed the labourer, "her heels are where her head ought to be!"

"It is really a horrid chasm," said the virtuoso, peeping into the ditch.

"Every body, from the highest to the lowest, have their ups and downs in this world," observed a lame beggarman, with a malicious smile.

Having seated the lady upon the bank, and put every thing to rights, Sophia joined us, and with the help of a smelling bottle, and chafing the lady's temples, she was restored to herself; she had received but little injury that we could perceive, and she declared she felt none. "But I fear I shall be thrown out," said the lady; so courtesying to Sophia, and smiling thanks to O'Carrol and myself, with our help, she mounted her hunter, cleared the ditch where she was thrown, and taking a short cut, to avoid the impending evil, was soon out of sight, and we returned to the cottage.

SPORTING IN THE UNITED STATES.
From " A Year's Residence," &c. by W. Cobbet.

There cannot be said to be any thing here which we, in England, call hunting. The deer are hunted by dogs indeed, but the hunters do not follow: they are posted at their several stations to shoot the deer as he passes. This is only one remove from the Indian hunting. I never saw, that I know of, any man that had seen a pack of hounds in America, except those kept by old John Brown, in Buck's county, Pensylvania, who was the only hunting-Quaker that I ever heard of, and who was grandfather of the famous General Brown. In short, there is none of what we call hunting; or so little, that no man can expect to meet with it.

No coursing. I never saw a greyhound here. Indeed there are no hares that have the same manners that ours have, or any thing like their fleetness. The woods, too, or some sort of cover, except in the singular instance of plains in this island, are too near at hand.

But of shooting, the variety is endless. —Pheasants, partridges, woodcocks, snipes, grouse, wild ducks of many sorts, teal, plover, and rabbits. There is a disagreement between the north and the south, as to the naming of the former. North of New Jersey, the pheasants are called partridges, and the partridges are called quails. To the south of New Jersey, they are called by what I think their proper names—taking the English names of those birds to be proper. For pheasants do not remain in covies, but mix like common fowls. The intercourse between the males and females is promiscuous, and not by pairs, as in the case of partridges; and these are the manners of the American pheasants, which are found by ones, twos, and so on, and never in families, except when young, when, like chickens, they keep with the old hen.

The American partridges are not quails, because quails are gregarious: they keep in flocks like rooks (called crows in America;) or like larks or starlings. It is a well known fact that quails flock; it is also well known, that partridges do not, but that they keep in distinct families, which we call covies, from the French covee, which means the eggs or brood which a hen covers at one time. The American partridges live in covies. The cock and hen pair in the spring. They have their brood by sitting alternately on the eggs, just as the English partridges do, the young ones, if none are killed or die, remain with the old ones till Spring. The covey always live within a small distance of the same spot; if frightened into a state of separation, they call to each other and re-assemble; they roost altogether in a round ring, as close as they can sit, the tails inward and the heads outward, and are in short, in all their manners, precisely the same as the English partridge, with this exception, that they will sometimes alight on a rail or a bough; and that when the hen sits, the cock, perched at a little distance, makes a sort of periodical whistle, in a monotonous, but very soft and sweet tone. The size of the pheasant is about the half of that of the English. The plumage is by no means so beautiful, but the flesh is far more delicate. The size of the partridge bears about the same proportion, but its plumage is more beautiful than that of the English, and its flesh more delicate. Both are delightful, though rather difficult shooting. The pheasant does not tower, but darts through the trees; and the partridge does not ride boldly, but darts away at no great height from the ground. Some years they are more abundant than other years.

The woodcocks are, in all respects, like those in England, except that they are only about three-fifths of the size. They breed here; and are in such numbers, that some men kill twenty brace or more in a day. Their haunts are in marshy places or woods. The shooting of them lasts from the Fourth of July till the hardish frosts come. Here are five months of this sort; and pheasants and partridges are shot from September to April.

The snipes are called English snipes, which they resemble in all respects, and are found in great abundance in the usual haunts of snipes.

The grouse is precisely like the Scotch grouse. There is only here and there a place where they are found; but they are, in those places, killed in great quantities, in the fall of the year.

As to the wild ducks and other water-fowl, which are come at by lying in wait, and killed most frequently swimming or sitting, they are slaughtered in whole flocks. An American counts the cost of powder and shot. If he is deliberate in every thing else, this habit will hardly forsake him in the act of shooting.— When the sentimental flesh-eaters hear the report of his gun, they may begin to pull out their white handkerchiefs, for death follows his pull of the trigger, with perhaps even more certainty than it used to follow the lancet of Dr. Rush.

The plover is a fine bird, and is found in great numbers upon the plains, and in the cultivated fields of this island. Plovers are very shy and wary; but they have ingenious enemies to deal with. A wagon or carriage of some sort, is made use of to approach them; and then they are easily killed.

Rabbits are very abundant in some places. They are killed by shooting: for all here is done with the gun. No reliance is placed upon a dog.

As to the Game Laws, there are none, except those which appoint the time for killing. People go where they like, and as to wild animals shoot what they like. There is a common law, which forbids trespass; and the statute-law, I believe, of "malicious trespass," or trespass after warning; and these are more than enough; for nobody, that I ever heard of, warns people off: so that, as far as shooting goes, and that is the sport which is the most general favourite, there never was a more delightful country than this island. The sky is so fair, the soil so dry, the cover so convenient, the game so abundant, and the people, go where you will, so civil, hospitable and kind.

CHESS.

A plan to make the Knight move into all the squares of the Chess-board in succession, without passing twice over the same.

4	7	2	11	16	21	26	23
1	10	5	56	27	24	17	20
6	3	8	15	12	19	22	25
9	64	57	60	55	28	13	18
44	59	54	63	14	61	40	29
51	48	45	58	41	32	37	34
46	43	50	53	62	35	30	39
49	52	47	42	31	38	33	36

It is obvious, the motion may be continued, or begun at any square *ad libitem.*

To a player the moves must be so evident,

that in a few trials, he will write the figures down upon a piece of paper, with the same facility as if he were writing his name.

Dr. Hutton, in his "Mathematical Recreations," gives three different methods to perform the same, but none of them like the above.

BADGER-HUNTING.

The badger is not known to exist in hot countries; it is an original native of the temperate climates of Europe, and is found, without any variety in Spain, France, Italy, Germany, Britain, Poland, and Sweden. It breeds only twice in a year, and brings forth four or five at a time. The usual length of the badger is somewhat above two feet, exclusive of the tail, which is about six inches long; its eyes are small, and are placed in a black stripe, which begins behind the ears, and runs tapering towards the nose: the throat and legs are black; the back, sides, and tail are of a dirty gray, mixed with black; the legs are very short, strong, and thick; each foot consists of five toes; those on the fore feet are armed with strong claws, well adapted for digging its subterraneous habitation.

The badger retires to the most secret recesses, where it digs its hole, and forms its habitation under ground. Its food consists chiefly of roots, fruits, grass, insects, and frogs. It is accused of destroying lambs and rabbits; but there seems to be no other reason for considering it as a beast of prey, than the analogy between its teeth, and those of carnivorous animals.

Few creatures defend themselves better, or bite with greater keenness than the badger; on that account it is frequently baited with dogs trained for that purpose, and defends itself from their attacks with astonishing agility and success. Its motions are so quick, that a dog is often desperately wounded in the moment of assault, and obliged to fly. The thickness of the badger's skin, and the length and coarseness of its hair, are an excellent defence against the bites of the dogs: its skin is so loose as to resist the impression of their teeth, and gives the animal an opportunity of turning itself round, and wounding its adversaries in their tenderest parts. In this manner this singular creature is able to resist repeated attacks both of men and dogs, from all quarters; till, being overpowered with numbers, and enfeebled by many desperate wounds, it is at last obliged to yield.

In hunting the badger, you must seek the earths and burrows where he lies; and, in a clear moonlight night, go and stop all the burrows except one or two, and therein place some sacks, fastened with drawing strings, which may shut him in as soon as he strains the bag. Some only place a hoop in the mouth of the sack, and so put it into the hole; and as soon as the badger is in the sack, and strains it, the sack slips from the hoop, and secures him in it, where he lies trembling till he is taken from his prison.

The sacks, or bags, being thus set, cast off the hounds, beating about all the woods, hedges, and tufts, round about for the compass of a mile or two; and what badgers are abroad, being alarmed by the hounds, will soon betake themselves to their burrows. Observe, that the person who is placed to watch the sacks, must stand close, and upon a clear wind; otherwise the badger will discover him, and immediately fly some other way into his burrow.

But if the dogs can encounter him before he can take his sanctuary, he will then stand at bay like the boar, and make good sport; vigourously biting and clawing the dogs. In general when they fight, they lay on their backs, using both teeth and nails; and, by blowing up their skins defend themselves against the bites of the dogs, and the blows given by the men. When the badger finds that the terriers yearn* him in his burrow, he will stop the hole betwixt him and the terriers; and, if they still continue baying, he will remove his couch into another chamber or part of the burrow, and so from one to another barricading the way before them, as he retreats, till he can go no farther.

If you intend to dig the badger out of his burrow, you must be provided with such tools as are used for digging out a fox: you should

* To yearn, is to bark as beagles do at their prey.

also have a pail of water to refresh the terriers when they come out of the earth to take breath and cool themselves.

It is no unusual thing to put some small bells about the necks of the terriers which making a noise, will cause the badger to bolt out.

In digging, the situation of the ground must be observed and considered; or, instead of advancing the work, you probably may hinder it.

In this order you may besiege them in their holds, or castles, and break their platforms, parapets, and casements; and work to them with mines and countermines, till you have overcome them.

We must do this animal the justice to observe, that, though nature has furnished it with formidable weapons of offence, and has besides given it strength sufficient to use them with great effect, it is, notwithstanding, very harmless and inoffensive, and, unless attacked, employs them only for its support.

The badger is an indolent animal, and sleeps much: it confines itself to its hole during the whole day, and feeds only in the night. It is so cleanly as never to defile its habitation with its odure. Immediately below the tail between that and the anus, there is a narrow transverse orifice, from whence a white substance, of a foetid smell, constantly exudes. The skin, when dressed with the hair on, is used for pistol furniture. Its flesh is eaten; the hind quarters are sometimes made into hams, which, when cured, are not inferior in goodness to the best bacon. The hairs are made into brushes, which are used by painters to soften and harmonize their shades.

In walking, the badger treads on his whole heel, like the bear, which brings its belly very near the ground.

A MAN ATTACKED BY WEASELS.

In the month of December, 1817, in the parish of Glencairn, a labourer was suddenly attacked by six weasels, which rushed upon him from an old dyke, in the field where he was at work. The man, alarmed at such a furious onset from an unprovoked enemy, instantly betook himself to flight, in which, however he was closely pursued, and although he had about him a large horse-whip, with which he endeavoured by several back-handed strokes to stop them, yet so eager was their pursuit, that he was on the point of being seized by the throat, when he luckily noticed at some distance, the fallen branch of a tree, which he made for, and hastily snatching it up, commenced in turn the attack with so much success, that he killed three of them, and put the remaining three to flight. The man's life was in great danger, when it is ascertained that two weasels are a match for a dog.

COURAGE OF THE STAG.
By Capt. Smith.

It is worthy of remark that the native courage of the stag has often formed an interesting topic of inquiry; and the following Indian anecdote shows that when pressed by enemies, he possesses it in an eminent degree. As Captain Smith, of the Native Infantry, and some friends were on a shooting party, very early in the morning, they observed a tiger steal out of a jungle, in pursuit of a herd of deer; having selected his object, the poor animal was quickly deserted by the herd; the tiger advanced with such amazing swiftness, that the stag in vain attempted to escape, and at the moment the gentlemen expected to see the tiger take the fatal spring, the stag gallantly faced his enemy, and for some minutes kept him at bay, and it was not till after three attacks, that the tiger secured his prey. He was supposed to have been considerably injured by the horns of the stag, as, on the advance of Captain Smith, he abandoned the carcase of the stag, having only sucked the blood from the throat.

It is not more than fifty years ago that the following experiment was made by his Royal Highness the late Duke of Cumberland, to ascertain the true and natural instinctive courage of the stag, when opposed to an enemy of the most formidable and terrific description.

To effect this, one of the ablest stags in Windsor forest was enclosed in an area formed upon a selected spot near the lodge, and surrounded with a remarkably strong net toiling, full fifteen feet high; and this ceremony took place in sight of Ascoth Heath races, so that thousands were present upon the occasion. When every thing was prepared, and the stag parading in majestic consternation at the astonishing assemblage of people around the net work, at the awful moment, when it may be naturally conceived, every heart beat high, with wonder, fear, and expectation, a trained ounce, or hunting tiger, was led in, hoodwinked, by the two blacks that had the care of him, and who, upon signal, set him and his eyes at liberty. Perhaps so general a silence never prevailed among so many thousands of spectators, as at that moment, when the slightest aspiration of a breeze might have been distinctly heard. The tiger, taking one general survey, instantly caught sight of the deer, and crouching down on his belly, continued to creep exactly in the manner of a cat drawing up to a mouse, watching to dart upon his prey with safety. The stag, however, most warily, steadily, and sagaciously, turned as he turned; and this strange and desperate antagonist found himself dangerously opposed by the threatenings of his formidable brow antlers. In vain did the tiger attempt every manœuvre to turn his flanks—the stag possessed too much generalship to be foiled upon the terra firma of his native country by a foreign invader. This cautious warfare continuing so long as to render it tedious, and probably to protract the time of starting the horses upon the race ground, his Royal Highness inquired if, by irritating the tiger, the catastophre of the combat might not be hastened. He was answered it might probably prove dangerous, or be attended with disagreeable consequences; but it was directed to be done: upon which the keepers proceeded very near the tiger, and did as they were ordered: when, immediately, without attacking the deer, with a most furious and elastic bound, he sprung at and cleared the toiling that enclosed them; landing amidst the clamours, shouts, and affrighted screams of the multitude, who fled in every direction, each, male and female, thinking themselves the destined victim of the tiger's rage; who, nevertheless, regardless of their fears or their persons, crossed the road, and rushed into the opposite wood, where he fastened upon the haunch of one of the fallow-deer, and brought him to the ground. His keepers, to whom he was perfectly familiarized, hesitated for some time to go near him; at length, however, they mustered resolution to approach, and cutting the deer's throat, separated the haunch, which he had seized, and led him away with it in his mouth.

AN ORIGINAL INVITATION SPORTING CARD.

BOXIANA

Most respectfully invites the *Lads of the Fancy* to assist him

On Tuesday Evening, Feb. 2. 1819.

At BEN MEDLEY'S,

The Canterbury Arms, near the Marsh Gate,

LAMBETH,

To *floor* Dull Care, should he dare intrude—get the best of Animosity, to prevent his *cross* mug from even taking a peep—and to knock down Discord, *sans ceremonie*, if he interrupt the sociality of the meeting.

THE RING

will be cleared, and the *setts-to* commence precisely at

EIGHT o'clock.

An excellent trial of skill is expected between Harmony and Good Humour, who, at present, are both backed at even; but it is rather anticipated, by the good judges, that Harmony will take the lead.

Those experienced heroes, *Messieurs Serious* and *Comic Songs*, have offered their services to officiate as seconds upon this occasion.

And the bottle holders (acknowledged as nothing else but good ones) will in case their men want recruiting supply them with Eau d'Vie, and the regular brilliant Daffy, or heavy wet, if it is preferred.

A spirited *turn-up* is also expected, between Messrs. *Duetts, Glees,* and *Recitations.*

The Umpire is Liberality; the Time-Keeper, " Fly not yet! Oh stay!" and

THE PRESIDENT (BOXIANA)

will exert himself to keep the *game* alive, according to the acceptation of the Poet, that

"*The right end of Life is to live and be jolly.*"

N. B. The Members and Chairman of the Daffy Club, have promised to attend the meeting, to put the company in *spirits.*

†↓† No *Gloves* can be permitted to be introduced upon this occasion, except the weather pleads for their appearance.

Minute time allowed.

ANECDOTES OF THE LATE LORD ORFORD.

No man ever sacrificed so much time, or so much property on practical or speculative sporting as the late Earl of Orford, whose eccentricities are too firmly indented upon "the tablet of memory," ever to be obliterated from the diversified rays of retrospection. Incessantly engaged in the pursuit of sport and new inventions, he introduced more whimsicalities, more experimental genius, and enthusiastic zeal, than any man yet did before him, or most probably any other man ever may attempt to do again.

Among his experiments of fancy, was a determination to drive four red-deer stags in a phaeton instead of horses, and these he had reduced to perfect discipline for his excursions and short journeys upon the road: but unfortunately, as he was one day driving to Newmarket their ears were saluted with the cry of a pack of hounds, which soon after crossing the road in the rear caught the scent of the "four in hand," and commenced a new kind of chase, with "breast high" alacrity. The novelty of this scene was rich beyond description; in vain did his lordship exert all his charioteering skill; in vain did his well-trained grooms energetically endeavour to ride before them: reins, trammels, and the weight of the carriage, were of no effect, for they went with the celerity of a whirlwind; and this modern Phaeton, in the midst of his electrical vibrations of fear, bid fair to experience the fate of his namesake. Luckily however, his Lordship had been accustomed to drive this set of "fiery-eyed steeds" to the Ram Inn, at Newmarket, which was most happily at hand, and to this his Lordship's most fervent prayers and ejaculations had been ardently directed; into the yard they suddenly bounded, to the dismay of ostlers and stable boys, who seemed to have lost every faculty upon the occasion. Here they were luckily overpowered, and the stags, the phaeton, and his lordship were all instantaneously huddled together in a barn, just as the hounds appeared in full cry at the gate.

TO THE MEMORY OF SNOWBALL, A CELEBRATED GREYHOUND, THE PROPERTY OF MAJOR TOPHAM.

By W. UPTON.

SNOWBALL, what dog e'er gained a greater name?
  Scarce one; for swifter never ran than thee;
And dear to mem'ry as thou art to fame,
  Will coursers prize OLD SNOWBALL's *pedigree.*

Young *Wander* gaz'd to see thee scour the field,
  While the loud " Bravo!" spoke from ev'ry tongue!
Alas! poor hare, thy breath of life was seal'd,
  When SNOWBALL's footsteps on thy presence hung

Fleet dog! for matchless were thy deeds awhile,
  No greyhound ever did more worth combine,
And long like England's proud and matchless isle,
  Shall SNOWBALL's merits, like her glory, shine;

MODE OF TRAINING THE ARABIAN HORSE.
From M. Chateaubriand's Travels in Greece.

This interesting traveller thus accounts for the hardihood displayed by the Arabian horses.—They are never put under shelter, but left exposed to the most intense heat of the sun, tied by all four legs to stakes driven in the ground; so that they cannot stir. The saddle is never taken from their backs; they frequently drink but once, and have but one feed of barley in twenty-four hours. This rigid treatment, so far from wearing them out, gives them sobriety and speed. I have often admired an Arabian steed thus tied down to the burning sands, his hair loosely flowing, his head bowed between his legs to find a little shade; and stealing with his wild eye an oblique glance of his master. Release his legs from the shackles, spring upon his back, and he will paw in the valley, he will rejoice in his strength, he will swallow the ground in the fierceness of his rage; and you recognise the original of the picture delineated by Job. Eighty or one hundred piastres are given for an ordinary horse, which is in general less valued than an ass or mule; but a horse of a well known Arabian breed will fetch any price. Abdallah, Pacha of Damascus, had just given 3000 piastres for one. The history of a horse is frequently the topic of general conversation. When I was at Jerusalem, the feats of one of these steeds made a great noise. The Bedouin to whom the animal, a mare, belonging, being pursued by the Governor's Guards, rushed with her from the top of the hills that overlook Jericho.

The mare scoured at full gallop down an almost perpendicular declivity without stumbling, and left the soldiers lost in admiration and astonishment. The poor creature, however, dropped down dead on entering Jericho, and the Bedouin, who would not quit her, was taken weeping over the body of his companion. This mare has a brother in the desert, who is so famous, that the Arabs always know where he has been, where he is, what he is doing, and how he does. Ali Aga religiously showed me in the mountains near Jericho the footsteps of the mare that died in the attempt to save her master. A

Macedonian could not have beheld those of Bucephalus with greater respect.

ON THE USEFULNESS OF PUGILISM.
From Mr. Ryley's "Itinerant."

I was preparing to say "Good night," after handing the young lady down stairs at the Opera House, when her brother, with the pleasant freedom of an old acquaintance, pressed me to take a Sandwich in St. James's-street, and, as his sentiments, as far as they had been communicated, agreed with mine, I accepted his invitation with the same frankness with which it was made. The female between us, we proceeded along Pall-mall; and turning up St. James's-street, two men, apparently in a state of intoxication, reeled out of an entry, and attempted to seize hold of the lady, who at that moment was unguarded on the right hand, her brother being a few paces in the rear. The street, as far as we could distinguish, was unoccupied, not even the voice of a watchman interrupted the solemn silence; but the moon shone with resplendent lustre, and my new friend, alarmed by his sister's screams, with the swiftness of a feathered Mercury, flew along the pavement, and with one blow laid the foremost of our assailants in the kennel. I was the more surprised at this, because his stature did not exceed five feet, and from the view I had of him, I was not prepared for uncommon strength. Our enemies were seemingly tall, raw-boned coal heavers, and though one of them was for the moment rendered incapable, our case appeared so desperate that, to the lady's cries, I added a call for the watch; but my companion, nothing daunted, bade me take care of his sister, and fear nothing.—"For," continued he, "if I cannot manage such rascals as these, I deserve to be d—d." The second ruffian, seeing his fellow on the ground, resumed his sobriety, and aimed a blow at me, but in so clumsy a manner, that I not only avoided it, but preserved my fair charge from harm; on which our little champion rushed forward, received the blow on the point of his elbow, and returned another in the pit of the stomach, which so staggered the wretch, that he reeled several paces, and finally tumbled headlong into an area, at least three yards deep. What I have employed so many words in relating was the work of a moment; having taught his foes to bite the ground, our skilful champion seized hold of his sister's disengaged arm, and, not suffering the grass to grow under our feet, we arrived in safety at his house.

This anecdote will, I think, establish the usefulness of pugilism. Had my friend been as little knowing in the science as his adversaries, very dreadful might have been the consequences, because might, in that case, would have overcome right, unless the fellows would have had patience to wait till he ran home for his sword;

and then indeed he might have killed them in a gentleman-like manner.

Every thing has its uses, and its abuses. But though it be granted, shall we neglect the use because it may possibly bring the abuse along with it? I have heard declaimers against the science of bruising say, "that a knowledge of self-defence makes people quarrelsome." If I may speak, from very limited experience, I think the contrary. I was well acquainted with Perrins, and never in my life saw a more harmless, quiet, inoffensive being. I have the pleasure of knowing Gulley—yes, reader—the pleasure. I would rather know him than many Sir Billys, and Sir Dillys, and he is neither quarrelsome, turbulent, nor overbearing.

One evening I accompanied honest Jack Emery to a tavern in Carey-street, kept by John Gulley. As we passed along Emery said, "You conceive, I dare say, Romney, that I am going to introduce you into a society of rogues and pick-pockets, and if you can compound for the loss of your purse or handkerchief, it will be a lucky escape; but rest assured you are mistaken. Gulley's house is, of course, open to all descriptions, but the majority of his customers are people of reputation and respectability."

This account, I confess, was some relief to my mind, where a considerable degree of prejudice existed against prize-fighters, and the houses they frequent. Gulley was unfortunately from home, but Crib, the Champion of England, was officiating as his locum tenens, and handing about pots of porter and grog with persevering industry. Mrs. Gulley, a neat little woman, civil and attentive, superintended the business of the bar; where, through Emery's interest, for I found he was in high favour, we obtained leave to sit. Crib uncorked and decanted, but could not give us his company, (which to me, as a noviciate in such scenes, would have been a treat,) owing to the business of the house, which he seemed to pursue much to his master's interest. Crib, who had obtained popularity by his prowess, was originally a coal-heaver, and has several brothers in the same employment; he is sturdy and stout built, about five and twenty, stands five feet eight inches, clumsy in appearance, rather hard featured, with a profile not unlike Cooke the tragedian. He is, I believe, a good-natured quiet fellow, and after we had detained him a few minutes in conversation—" Well," said Emery, " what do you think of the greatest man in his way, or perhaps any other, can boast? for Gulley has altogether declined the business."

" Why, to speak the truth, notwithstanding your caution, I expected, in a house kept and frequented by boxers, to have seen nothing but blackguards, and to have heard nothing but blasphemy; but I am so pleasingly deceived, and so comfortably situated, that I believe this will not be the last visit I shall pay Mrs. Gulley, and as to the Champion of England, I can only wonder how a person of his apparently good disposition can ever be wrought up to wound, to lame, perhaps to kill his adversary. And how is it that people can meet in this manner without any cause of quarrel? Is it glory that stirs them on? Can ambition so far stimulate a man, that he shall be dead to sense of pain, and callous to personal suffering? It must be so, for a meeting of this kind is so truly a matter of business, that previous to the most fierce and determined battles, the parties shake hands as a proof of amity, and this is the signal for black eyes and bloody noses."

"Come, come Romney," said Emery, "I brought you here to be amused, and not to moralize; but since you are for the latter, we will e'en wish Mrs. Gulley good night."

JEALOUSY AND REVENGE OF A COCK.

The habitudes of the domestic breed of poultry cannot, possibly, escape observation; and every one must have noticed the fierce jealousy of the cock. It should seem that this jealousy is not confined to his rivals, but may, sometimes extend to his beloved female; and that he is capable of being actuated by revenge, founded on some degree of reasoning, concerning her conjugal infidelity. An incident which happened at the seat of Mr. B——, near Berwick, justifies this remark. "My mowers," (says he) "cut a partridge on her nest, and immediately brought the eggs (fourteen) to the house. I ordered them to be put under a very large beautiful hen, and her own to be taken away. They were hatched in two days, and the hen brought them up perfectly well till they were five or six weeks old. During that time they were constantly kept confined in an out-house, without having been seen by any of the other poultry. The door happened to be left open and the cock got in. My housekeeper, hearing her hen in distress, ran to her assistance, but did not arrive in time to save her life; the cock, finding her with the brood of partridges, fell upon her with the utmost fury, and put her to death. The housekeeper found him tearing her both with his beak and spurs, although she was then fluttering in the last agony, and incapable of any resistance. The hen had been, formerly, the cock's greatest favourite."

DEATH OF TOM MOODY.

The noted Whipper-in, well known to the Sportsmen of Shropshire.

You all know Tom Moody* the whipper-in well:
The bell just done tolling was honest Tom's knell;
A more able sportsman, ne'er followed a hound,
Thro' a country well known to him fifty miles round;
No hound ever open'd with Tom in the wood.

* The veteran sportsman, who is the subject of this ballad, died some years since, in the service of Mr. Forrester, of Shropshire. He had been the whipper-in to that gentleman's pack upwards of thirty years: and from the whimsical circumstances attending his burial, it is considered as worthy of a place in this collection.

But he'd challenge the tone, and could tell if 'twas good;
And all, with attention, would eagerly mark,
When he cheer'd up the pack—" Hark!
  To Rockwood, hark! hark!
  High?—Wind him? and cross him!
  Now Rattler, boy!—hark!"

Six crafty earth stoppers, in hunter's green drest
Supported poor Tom to an "earth" made for rest;
His horse, which he styl'd his " Old Soul," next appear'd,
On whose forehead the brush of his last fox was rear'd;
Whip, cap, boots, and spurs, in a trophy were bound,
And here and there follow'd an old straggling hound.
Ah! no more at his voice yonder vales will they trace!
Nor the wrekin* resound his first burst into the chase!
  "With high over!—Now press him!
  Tally-ho—tally-ho!"

Thus Tom spoke his friends, e'er he gave up his breath—
" Since I see you're resolved to be in at the death,
One favour bestow—'tis the last I shall crave—
Give a rattling view-halloo, thrice over my grave:
And unless at that warning I lift up my head,
My boys! you may fairly conclude I am dead!"
Honest Tom was obey'd, and the shout rent the sky,
For ev'ry voice join'd in the Tally-ho! cry.
  " Tally-ho!—Hark forwards!
  Tally-ho!—Tally-ho!"

OF THE QUALITIES OF THE GREYHOUND.
By a Sportsman of 1819.

It appears from a Welsh proverb† that a gentleman was known by his hawk, his horse, and his greyhound; and Mr. Pennant‡ has observed by a law of Canute, a greyhound was not to be kept by a person inferior to a gentleman.

---

* The famous mountain in Shropshire.

† Wrth ei walch, ei farche, a'i filgi, yr adwaenir donhaddig. Pennant.

‡ British Zoology vi. 1. p. 53.

The different perfections of the greyhound, it seems, have been comprised in the following rude and barbarous rhymes:—

> The head like a snake;
> The neck like a drake;
> The back like a beam;
> The side like a bream;
> The tail like a rat;
> The foot like a cat.

Ludicrous as this poetical effort may be, the description is still correct; and these different qualities, when united, even now form the model of perfection in the race. On the superior breed of greyhounds, there has been a variety of opinions: the blood of the late Lord Orford's was allowed to stand very high, if not the first, in the public estimation. Perhaps there has not been any person who took more pains to arrive at the utmost state of perfection in his object; and it is a circumstance generally believed, that he even had recourse to a cross with the English bull-dog, in order to acquire a courage and resolution till then unknown. After seven descents, it is said, he obtained the object for which he had been so solicitous, without any diminution of speed, or the beauties of shape and symmetry. Lord River's stock is now allowed to be one of the first in England, and its superiority may be owing to a judicious cross of the Dorsetshire and Newmarket blood. Mr. Gurney of Norwich, has likewise for some years been in possession of a breed in considerable repute. It has the three great requisites, blood, bone, and shape. Snowdrop, a son of Snowball, won the Malton cup four successive years; and Fly, a grand-daughter of Major Topham, carried it away also in the Malton Spring Meeting of 1810, though she had suffered previously by very severe exercise. Scarcely a greyhound, indeed, of any other blood now appears at the Malton Meeting, and it has been so celebrated as to be introduced in almost every county in the kingdom.

There was a circumstance respecting Snowball peculiar to him in the history of coursing. He served greyhounds for years before his death at three guineas each. The first year had 10; the second, 14; the third, 11; and the fourth, 7. And amongst them, two out of Wales, two out of Scotland, one from the Marquis of Townshend, out of Norfolk, and the rest out of counties ot some distance. Fifty guineas were given for Young Snowball, who was sold afterwards for one hundred; and Mr. Mellish beat all Newmarket with another son of Snowball.

In the South, Millar, belonging to Sir H. B. Dudley, has been likewise very famous. The sire of Millar was an Essex dog, Tulip, by a blue Newmarket dog, and he was the produce of a bitch by a Lancashire dog bred by the late Mr. Bamber Gascoyne. Millar was a deep-chested dog, of a fawn colour, and whilst young did not discover any pretensions to his future reputation. He was afterwards tried in the Essex Marshes, and in a single day he beat no less than five of the first and best dogs in the field. His superiority continued for some years, and he won upwards of seventy matches. His stock also proved excellent runners, and Miss, one of his daughters, received the Bradwell cup from twelve opponents who had been run down to a brace. Whatever, therefore, may be thought by a few individuals on the subject, it is certain that blood has a very striking superiority.—Half-bred horses have been sometimes known to exhibit great speed and bottom; but in general a thorough-bred horse only can maintain and continue his velocity for miles in succession. The same observation may be made with respect to the greyhound, and it forms the essential difference, which is not often properly attended to, between the greyhound in an open and enclosed country. The coarse haired greyhound may discover some prowess in the latter; but in the former, and in long and severe courses, blood, which includes the shape, sets all competition at defiance.

On the propriety of breeding akin, in the sportsman's phrase, or from the same blood, there have been various opinions; but it appears to be a practice neither to be desired nor pursued with advantage. If continued for some litters, a manifest inferiority of size, and a deficiency of bone, will soon be visible, as well as a want of courage and bottom; though the beauty of the form, with the exception of the size, may not be diminished. If we are to believe Varro, there has been an instance even in the brute creation, of a repugnance to such conjunctions. By a judicious choice and an attention to the shape, blood, and bone of another stock, a cross may always be procured, which in general meet the sportsman's wishes; being attended with every advantage, without any of the consequences to be feared from a contrary practice, there can be little hesitation in adopting it.

The most favourable season for the production of the young brood, in the opinion of the ancients, was that of the warm months. If dogs are bred in the summer months, they will also be of the fittest age to be brought into the field the following year.

It is rather singular that no other alterations have been made in the "rules and laws of coursing" since the reign of Queen Elizabeth, when the Regulations, which are usually still in force received the fiat of Thomas, Duke of Norfolk, and are as follow:—

THE LAWS OF THE LEASH, OR COURSING;

As they were commanded, allowed, and subscribed, by Thomas, late Duke of Norfolk, in the Reign of Queen Elizabeth.

First, Therefore it was ordered, that he which was chosen fewterer, or letter-loose of the greyhounds, should receive the greyhounds match to run together into his leash as soon as he came into the field, and to follow next to the hare finder till he came unto the form; and no horseman nor footman, on pain of disgrace, to go before them, or on either side, but directly behind, the space of forty yards or thereabouts.

Item. That not above one brace of greyhounds do course a hare at one instant.

Item. That the hare-finder should give the hare three So-hows before he put her from her lear, to make the Greyhounds gaze and attend her rising.

Item. That dog that giveth first turn, if, after the turn be given, there be neither coat, slip, nor wrench, extraordinary, then he which gave the first turn shall be held to win the wager.

Item. If one dog give the first turn, and the other bear the hare, then he which bore the hare shall win.

Item. If one dog give both the first turn, and last turn, and no other advantage between them, that odd turn shall win the wager.

Item. The coat shall be more than two turns, and a go-by or the bearing of the hare, equal to two turns.

Item. If neither dog turn the hare, then he which leadeth last, at the covert, shall be held to win the wager.

Item. If one dog turn the hare, serve himself, and turn her again, those two turns shall be as much as a coat.

Item. If all the course be equal, then he only which bears the hare shall win; and if she be not borne, then the course must be adjudged dead.

Item. If any dog shall take a fall in the course, and yet perform his part, he shall challenge advantage of a turn more than he giveth.

Item. If one dog turn the hare, serve himself, and give divers coats, yet in the end stand still in the field, the other dog without turn-giving, running home to the covert, that dog which stood still in the field shall be then adjudged to lose the wager.

Item. If any man shall ride over a dog and overthrow him in his course (though the dog were the worst dog in opinion) yet the party for the offence shall either receive the disgrace of the field or pay the wager, for between the parties it shall be adjudged to cours.

Item. Those who are chosen judges of the leash, shall give their judgments presently before they depart from the field, or else he, in whose default it lieth, shall pay the wager by a general voice and sentence.

The substance of the above rules, it seems, has been adhered to in the sporting counties; but the dogs are now loosed out of a double spring-slip, which renders it impossible for either to have the advantage of the start. In Wiltshire, however, some judicious deviations have been introduced; and the dog that hath the best of the course, whether he kills the hare or not, is there declared to be the winner. The propriety of such a decision is apparent, for the best and speediest dog may turn the hare directly on his opponent, who may have no other merit than that of laying hold of his game when forced full upon him.

RUNNING IN A SACK.

In the month of November, 1811, a wager was run, for ten guineas a side, in White Conduit Fields, between two tradesmen of the names of Williams and Johnson, of the neighbourhood of Islington; the one was to run one hundred yards in a sack, in less space of time than the other should go twice the distance in the common may of running. A vast number of persons assembled to witness the novelty, and a great many bets were depending upon the issue; odds were three to one against Williams in the sack. They started at four o'clock; almost directly afterwards the man in the sack fell down, and the other by some accident tumbled over him, and they both scrambled to get up; the former though in the sack, being the most active, recovered himself first, and won the wager by about twenty seconds.

MOST EXTRAORDINARY PERFORMANCE ACCOMPLISHED WITH A BAROUCHE.

A party of gentlemen, on Tuesday, the 10th of March, 1812, for a considerable wager, started from the George Inn, at Portsmouth, in Bellet's Barouche-and-four, to reach London, a distance of seventy-two miles, in seven hours and three-quarters; which to the astonishment of both parties, was accomplished in five hours and thirty-one minutes, being two hours and fourteen minutes less than the given time; averaging fourteen miles an hour. The following is a statement of the distance, and places of changing horses.

	Miles.	Min.
From Portsmouth to Horndean	10	53
— to Petersfield	8	32
— to Liphook	8	41
— to Godalming	12	54
— to Ripley	10	47
— to Kingston	12	45
— to Hyde Park Corner	12	49
Changing of the horses		10
	72	331

FALCONRY AMONG THE ANCIENTS.

An early writer on this subject gives us the following anecdote:—"I once had (says he) an excellent opportunity of seeing this sport near Nazareth in Galilee. An Arab, mounting a swift courser, held the falcon on his hand, as huntsmen commonly do. When he espied the animal on the top of the mountain, he let loose the falcon, which flew in a direct line, like an arrow and attacked the antelope, fixing the talons of one of his feet into its cheeks, and those of the other into his throat, extending his wings obliquely over the animal; spreading one towards one of his ears, and the other to the opposite hip. The creature, thus attacked, made a leap twice the height of a man, and freed himself from the falcon; but, being wounded, and losing both its strength and speed, it was again attacked by the bird, which fixed the talons of both his feet into its throat, and held it fast, till the huntsmen coming up, took it alive, and cut its throat. The falcon was allowed to drink the blood, as a reward for his labour; and a young falcon, which was learning, was likewise put to the throat. By this means the young birds are taught to fix their talons in the throat of the animal, as the properest part: for, should the falcon fix upon the creature's hip, or some other part of the body, the huntsman would not only lose his game, but his falcon too; for the beast roused by the wound, which could not prove mortal, would run to the deserts and the tops of the mountains, whither its enemy, keeping its hold, would be obliged to follow, and being separated from its master, must of course perish.

SPORTING ADVENTURE OF COURTEOUS KING JAMIE.

By M. G. Lewis, Esq.

Courteous King Jamie is gone to the wood,
   The fattest buck to find;
He chased the deer, and he chased roe,
   Till his friends were left behind.

He hunted over moss and moor,
   And over hill and down,
Till he came to a ruined hunting hall
   Was seven miles from a town.

He entered up the hunting hall
   To make him goodly cheer,
For of all the herds in the good greenwood,
   He had slain the fairest deer.

He sat him down with food and rest
   His courage to restore,
When a rising wind was heard to sigh,
   And an earthquake rock'd the floor.

And darkness cover'd the hunting hall
   Where he sat all at his meat;
The gray dogs howling left their food
   And crept to Jamie's feet.

And louder howl'd the rising storm,
   And burst the fasten'd door,
And in there came a grisly Ghost,
   Loud stamping on the floor.

Her head touch'd the roof-tree of the house,
   Her waist a child could span;
I wot, the look of her hollow eye
   Would have scared the bravest man.

Her locks were like snakes, and her teeth like snakes,
   And her breath had a brimstone smell:
I know of nothing that she seem'd to be
   But the *Devil* just come from *Hell!*

"Some meat! some meat! King Jamie,
  Some meat now give to me."—
"And to what meat in this house, lady,
  Shall ye not welcome be?"
"Oh! ye must kill your berry-brown steed;
  And serve him up to me."

King Jamie has kill'd his berry-brown steed;
  Though it caused him mickle care;
The ghost eat him up both flesh and bone;
  And left nothing but hoofs and hair!

"More meat! more meat, King Jamie,
  More meat now give to me."
"And to what meat in this house, lady,
  Shall ye not welcome be?"
"Oh! ye must kill your good greyhounds;
  They'll taste more daintily."

King Jamie has kill'd his good greyhounds,
  Though it made his heart to fail:
The ghost eat them all up one by one,
  And left nothing but ears and tail.

"A bed! a bed, King Jamie,
  Now make a bed for me!"
"And to what bed in this house, lady,
  Shall ye not welcome be?"
"Oh! ye must pull the heather so green;
  And make a soft bed for me."

King Jamie has pull'd the heather so green
  And made for the ghost a bed;
And over the heather, with courtesy rare,
  His plaid has he daintily spread.

"Now swear! now swear! King Jamie,
  To take me for your bride;"—
"Now heaven forbid!" King Jamie said,
  That ever the like betide;
That the Devil so foul, just come from Hell,
  Should stretch him by my side!"

"Now fy! now fy! King Jamie,
  I swear by the holy tree,
I am no devil or evil thing,
  However foul I be.

"Then yield! then yield! King Jamie,
  And take my bridegroom's place;
For shame shall light on the dastard knight
  Who refuses a lady's grace."

"Then," quoth King Jamie with a groan,
  For his heart was big with care,
"It shall never be said, that King Jamie,
  Denied a lady's prayer."

So he laid him by the foul thing's side,
  And piteously he moan'd;
She press'd his hand, and he shuddered!
  She kiss'd his lips, and he groan'd?

When day was come, and night was gone,
  And the sun shone through the hall,
The fairest lady that ever was seen
  Lay between him and the wall!

"Oh! well is me!" King Jamie cried,
  "How long will your beauty stay?"
Then out and spake that lady fair,
  "E'en 'till my dying day.

"For I was witch'd to a ghastly shape,
  All by my step-dame's skill,
Till I could light on a courteous knight
  Who would let me have all my will!"

GIGANTIC CHALLENGE.

A Russian Anecdote.

During his reign, Wladimir had many wars to sustain, particularly against the Petchenegians. In one of the incursions of these people, the two armies were on the eve of a battle, being only separated by the waters of the Troubeje, when their prince advanced and proposed to terminate the difference by single combat between two champions; the people whose combatant should be overcome, not to take up arms against the other nation for three years.

The Russian sovereign accepted the proposal, and they reciprocally engaged to produce their champions. Among the troops of the Petchenegians was a man of an athletic make and colossal stature, who, vain of his strength, paced the bank of the river, loading the Russians with every species of insult, and provoking them by threatening gestures to enter the lists with him, at the same time ridiculing their timidity. The soldiers of Wladimir long submitted to these insults; no one offered himself to the encounter, the gigantic figure of their adversary terrifying the whole of them. The day of combat being arrived, they were obliged to supplicate for longer time.

At length an old man approached Wladimir; —"My lord," said he, "I have five sons, four of whom are in the army; as valiant as they are, none of them is equal to the fifth, who possesses prodigious strength." The young man was immediately sent for. Being brought before the prince, he asked permission to make a public trial of his strength. A vigorous bull was irritated with red hot irons: the young

Russian stopped the furious animal in his course, threw him to the ground, and tore his skin and flesh. This proof inspired the greatest confidence. The hour of battle arrives; the two champions advance between the camps, and the Petchenegian could not restrain a contemptuous smile when he observed the apparent weakness of his adversary, who was yet without a beard; but being quickly attacked with as much impetuosity as vigour, crushed between the arms of the young Russian, he is stretched expiring in the dust. The Petchenegians, seized with terror, took to flight; the Russians pursued, and completely overthrew them.

The sovereign loaded the conqueror, who was only a simple courier, with honours and distinctions. He was raised, as well as his father, to the rank of the grandees, and to preserve the remembrance of this action, the prince founded the city of Pereisaslavle on the field of battle, which still holds a distinguished rank among those of the government of Kiof.

NEITHER WON NOR LOST.—A WAGER.

The Bucks had dined, and deep in council sat,
Their wine was brilliant, but their wit grew flat:
Upstarts his Lordship, to the window flies,
And lo, " a race, a race," in rapture cries.
" Where?" quoth Sir John—" Why see, two drops of rain
Start from the summit of the crystal pane:
A thousand pounds, which drop with nimblest force,
Performs its current down the slippery course."

The bets were fix'd in dire suspense they wait
For victory pendant on the nod of fate.
Now down the sash, unconscious of the prize
The bubbles roll, like tears from Chloe's eyes!
But, ah, the glittering joys of life are short.
How oft two jostling steeds have spoil'd the sport!
So thus attraction by coercive laws,
Th' approaching drops into one bubble draws;
Each curs'd his fate, that thus their project crost,
How hard their lot who neither won nor lost!

THE RULING PASSION.

The late celebrated trainer, Frost, belonged to Sir Charles Bunbury, among many others trained that favourite mare, called Eleanor. During his last moments Sir Charles sent a clergyman to attend him; amidst his ejaculations Frost called out for Tom, (meaning one of the stable boys;) of course a pause ensued, as the clergyman supposed he was going to unburden his mind. When Tom came to his bedside, Frost shook him by the hand, and exclaimed, "Was not Eleanor a rum one?"

LUDICROUS ANGLING ANECDOTES.

Sir John Hawkins, in his notes on the Complete Angler, relates the following story:—"A lover of angling told me, he was fishing in the river Lea, at the ferry called Jeremy's, and had hooked a large fish at the time when some Londoners, with their horses, were passing. They congratulated him on his success, and got out of the ferry boat; but, finding the fish not likely to yield, mounted their horses, and rode off. The fact was, that angling for small fish, his bait had been taken by a barbel, too large for the fisher to manage. Not caring to risk his tackle by attempting to raise him, he hoped to tire him, and for that purpose suffered himself to be led, (to use his own expression) as a blind man is by a dog, several yards up, and as many down the bank of the river; in short, for so many hours, that the horsemen above-mentioned, who had been at Walthamstow and dined, were returned, who, seeing him thus occupied, cried out, "What, master, another large fish?" 'No,' says the Piscator, 'the very same.' 'Nay,' says one of them, that can never be; for it is five hours since we crossed the river.!" and, not believing him, they rode on their way. At length our angler determined to do that which a less patient one would have done long before: he made one vigorous effort to land the fish, broke his tackle, and lost him."

The same intelligent knight furnishes us with another anecdote relating to this sullen fish:— "Living some years ago," says he, " in a village on the banks of the Thames, I was used, in the summer months, to be much in a boat on the river; it happened, that at Shepperton, where I had been for a few days, I frequently passed an elderly gentleman in his boat, who appeared to be fishing at different stations for barbel. After a few salutations had passed between us, and we were become a little acquainted, I took occasion to inquire of him what diversion he had met with. 'Sir,' says he, 'I have but bad luck today; for I fish for barbel, and you know they are not to be caught like gudgeons.' 'Very true,' answered I,' 'but what you want in tale I suppose you make up in weight.' 'Why, sir,' replied he, 'that is just as it happens; I like the sport, and love to catch fish; but my great delight is in going after them. I'll tell you what, sir,' continued he, 'I am a man in years, and have been used to the sea all my life; (he had been an India captain) but I mean to go no more, and have bought that little house which you see there, (pointing to it) for the sake of fishing: I get into this boat (which he was then mopping) on a Monday morning, and fish on till Saturday night, for barbel, as I told you, for that is my delight; and this I have sometimes done for a month together, and all that while have not had one bite!'"

AERIAL COMBAT.

True courage, it should seem, is insensible to danger, as may be seen from the following circumstance. In July 1818, a mason and a labourer, both men of prowess, quarrelled on the scaffolding of the spire erected on the tower of the New Church of Newry, in Ireland. A pugilistic encounter took place, and the two fearless combatants fought near the summit of the unfinished building, where it was not quite a yard in diameter. The scaffolding and railing which encircle it, include a space of about eighty inches in diameter, and here the champions buffeted each other lustily at the height of one hundred and seventy-six feet above the surface of the ground. Some knock-down blows were given and received; but fortunately neither of the warriors were thrown out of the ring, or, as the technical phrase is, over the ropes. It is indeed to be feared, that, if they had been precipitated to mother earth, she would not have received them so kindly as she did her favourite son Antæus. The only men in modern times, who have equalled these genuine successors of Hercules, Eryx, and Eutellus, were Massena and Suwarrow, who fought in the Swiss mountains, three fourths of a mile above the cloud, and saw the lightning break, and heard the thunder roll, full many a fathom below the scene of action.

CURIOUS DEFINITION OF THE TITLE OF "A MAN OF THE WORLD."

One who has ruined the woman who loved him, and then abandoned her to shame, reproach, and penury—One who has shot his man, in what is deemed honourable warfare—One who has imposed on the trusting confidence of him he denominated his best friend, by ruining his fortune at the gaming table and then by way of a finish, eloping with the wife of his bosom—One who has broken the hearts of his parents, by raising the heedful at a premium of *cent. per cent.* upon the ancient estate of his more prudent forefathers, by granting to the money-lending sharks, bonds, post-obits, and mortgages, to be paid at the death of his sire. This desiratum gained, he flies to the club, sets on the hazard of a die the cultivated meadows, druidical oaks, and the gothic domains of his progenitors: seven's the main; he loses, and the antique towers of his family mansion tremble to their foundation—One who has wasted his inheritance; but who has purchased worldly wisdom; and the simple well plucked pigeon becomes transmuted, by dire necessity, to procure a livelihood, into a wily wary *Rook*, thus denominated—A MAN OF THE WORLD!

THE OLD ENGLISH HUNTSMAN AND MOLE-CATCHER.

By Mr. PRATT.

I must now beg you to accompany me to the hut of an ancient man; nor shall I make an apology for the liberty I take with you, since you liberally allow, I have more than once convinced you that places the least productive of scenic beauty, and the least distinguished in the map of the world, are the most favourable to the lover of his kind, and to the examiner of human nature. If it be true, that

> Full many a flower is born to blush unseen;

It is the business of the moral florist, or, shall we rather say, of the mental botanist, to take care that every specimen of nature's noblest blooms and plants shall not

> Waste their sweetness in the desert air.

Instead, then, of asking your pardon, let me demand your thanks, for now leading you over the unsheltered heath and open fields from Woodhurst to Warboys. There, passing a hamlet, let me conduct you along the dreary moor, cold, and comfortless as it is, but which supplies with many a warm sensation the peasant's hearth with peat, turf, and other cottage fuel of the fenland poor.

Reared of those turfs, on a few poles by way of pillars, and here and there a rude lath to fence the sides, and to form the door-way, behold a sort of hermit-seeming hovel. Yet it is not the abode of an anchoret: it is the daily retirement of a social old man, aged ninety-three years, whose name is John Grounds. He has followed the occupation of mole catcher forty of those years, gaining from the parish the sum of two pence for the capture of each mole; and, so uninterrupted has been his health, that he has not been prevented in his employment more than thrice in the whole of that long space of time, though the walk from his cottage at Warboys to his turf hovel on the moor, is a full English league, and most of his time passed upon marshy land, amidst humidity and vapours. Yet how few people who live in the air of a palace, and in the bosom of luxury, can vie with our poor fenlander, in all that makes life desirable—health, spirits, and content.

But having shown you his place of business by day, I will re-conduct you to the hut where he has passed the nights of those forty years in unbroken repose; and as we bend our way to the spot, I will present you with a true portrait of the man, and a brief sketch of his family, and of his adventures.

John Grounds, about sixty years preceding the date of this letter, had been a follower of my father's hounds, and distinguished himself as a lover of the sport; to partake of which, he would bound over the interposing fields, hedges, and ditches, with almost the speed, and more of the spirit, than the hounds themselves, upon the first summons of the bugle-horn. This early activity recommended him to the notice of the huntsman, who preferred him to the whipper-in-ship then vacant; and having, in this office, acquitted himself much to the satisfaction of the squire, and of the pack, which as he used to say, "all loved him to a dog," he was elevated, on the removal of his first patron, to another appointment, even to the entire command of the kennel: a situation which he filled for many years with great dignity and reputation. And although it was not till late in his reign I was of sufficient age to form any personal opinion of those achievements, which to the enthusiasts of the field-sports are reckoned as important as any which are appreciated by heroes of another description, in the field of battle—perhaps with more reason, certainly with less criminality, considering the general causes of war,—I was old enough before he resigned the canine sceptre, to attest, that his government exhibited that happy mixture of fortitude and moderation, encouraging the true, correcting the false, paying honour to the sagacious, and rearing up the young and thoughtless to steady excellence, at the same time punishing the babbler, and teaching the most ignorant. And I remember, I even then thought that poor John Grounds might furnish no mean model, whereby to form those who are destined to rule a more disorganized and extensive empire; and how often has this idea since occurred to me, as I traced back the events of my boyish days! That simple monarch of my father's kennel, thought I, might come forth in the blameless majesty of dominion, and dictate wisdom to ministers and kings.

The only poetical work wich my father seemed truly to enjoy, was Somerville's fine poem of the Chase, and often meeting it in my way, I perused and re-perused it with avidity; not so much from any love of its glorious subject, as my father often called it, nor because I caught any thing of the spirit which the music of bounds and of horn is said to inspire, for I was extremely degenerate in that respect, but because I seemed to be led over hills and dales, and scoured the plains, and followed the echoes through their woods, and brushed the dew, and passed the stream in company and under the muses. These appeared to show me the hare, her velocity and her energy, without worrying her. In numbers more harmonious than the sounds which were reverberated from the hills or thickets, these tuneful associates brought every thing of beauty and of sense to my mind's eye: and in reciting aloud different passages, that painted the loveliness of early morn, the fragrance of nature, the sagacity of the dog, and the pride of the horse, I was not seldom praised by my dear father, who thought me at length a convert to the joys and honours of the chase, when in effect I was only animated by the charms of verse; and I was complimented for my feelings being congenial with the sportsman, when in truth I was in raptures only with the poet.

As time warned my father of the necessity of relinquishing the vehement exercise connected with these diversions, John Grounds passed with a fair character into the service of Lady St. John of Bletsoe, as her Ladyship's gamekeeper, in which office he remained, in " goodly favour and liking," as he expressed it, till the sorrowful day of her death. After this he married, and lived well pleased till his first wife's decease;

but he found the holy estate so happy, that he entered upon it again : and jocosely now advises his second dame not to give him another opportunity, for fear the third time should not be so favourable.

This mole catching is united with the occupation of bird frighter, in those parts of the year when the feathered plunderers assault the corn or fruits; or when, as their poetical advocate observed, " the birds of heaven assert their right to, and vindicate their grain." But " poor fools," would Grounds often say, " I sometimes think they have as good a right to a plum, or a cherry, or a wheat-ear, as any Christian person; and so I seldom pop at them with any thing but powder; and that more for the pleasure of hearing the noise of the gun, than to do any execution; except now and then, indeed, I let fly at a rascally old kite, who would pounce upon cherry and bird too, and carry off one of my chicks into the bargain, if it lay in his way."

" And when I do try my hand at a thief, I am not often wide of my mark," cried the old man in a late interview; "I can still give him a leaden luncheon when I have a mind to it. Now and then, too, a carrion crow, with a murrain to him, and a long-necked heron, with a fish in his mouth, goes to pot: but somehow I don't relish fixing my trap for these poor soft creatures!" taking one from the mole-bag slung across his shoulders; " they look so comfortable and feel so soft and silky; and when they lay snugly under the earth, little thinking, poor souls! what a bait I have laid for them, seeing I cover the mumble-stick with fresh sod so slily, there seems to be no trap at all.—Though they turn up the ground to be sure, and rootle like so many little hogs; and for that matter do a power of mischief: and as for blindness, 'none are so blind as those who won't see,' your Honour. These fellows know a trap as well as I do, and can see my tricks as plain as I can see theirs: and sometimes they lead me a fine dance from hillock to hedge, with a murrain to them! pass through my traps, and after turning up an acre of ground, sometimes in a single night, give me the slip at last."

But it is time to look at the portrait of the man, and, lo! seated on a brown bench cut in the wall, within the chimney-place, in the corner of yon rude cottage, he presents himself to your view. Behold his still ruddy cheeks, his milk-white locks, partly curled and partly straight— see how correctly they are parted in the middle, almost to the division of a hair—a short pipe in his mouth—his dame's hand folded in his own— a jug of smiling beer warming in the wood ashes—a cheerful blaze shining upon two happy old countenances, in which, though you behold the indent of many furrows, they have been made by age, not sorrow—the good sound age of health, without the usual infirmities of long life, exhibiting precisely the unperceived decay so devoutly to be wished. On the matron's knee sits a purring cat; at the veteran's foot on the warm hearth, sleeps an aged hound of my father's breed, in the direct line of unpolluted descent; or, "a true chip of the old block," as John phrased it; and who, by its frequent and quick-repeated whaffle or demi-bark, seems to be dreaming of the chase. An antique gun is pendant over the chimney: a spinning-wheel occupies the vacant corner by the second brown bench: and a magpie, with closed eyes, and his bill nestled under his wing, is at profound rest in his wicket cage. To close the picture, the mole bag, half filled with the captives of the day, thrown into a chair, on which observe a kitten has clambered, and is in the act of playing with one of the soft victims, which it has contrived to purloin from the bag, for its pastime: while the frugal but sprightly light, from the well-stirred faggot, displays on the mud but clean walls, many a lime-embrowned ditty, as well moral as professional: such as—"God rest you, merry gentleman"—"The morning is up, and the cry of the hounds"—"The sportsman's delight"—"Chevy Chase"—and "The jolly huntsman."

Such exactly were persons and place, as in one of my visits of unfading remembrance to the good old folks, whom I had known in early days, I walked to Warboys, and surveyed its famous wood and fen.

But would you have a yet closer view of this happy, healthy, and innocent creature, who has passed near a century in blameless discharge of various employments, without having heaved one sigh of envy, or, as he told me, "shed one tear of sorrow, but when his parents died, or a friend and neighbour was taken away."

You must suppose you see him in his best array, when he walked three miles after having before walked three to his mole traps, "purposely, and in pure love," as he assured me, "to return my kind goodness with goodness in kind."

This happened at Woodhurst, and at the house of John Hills, from which my heart has already so successfully, as you tell me, addressed yours. The pencil of a painter from nature could never have had a happier opportunity of sketching from the life an old sportsman of England, in the habit of his country and his calling. It was no longer the little mole-catcher in his worsted gaiters and leathern deep-tanned jacket, sitting on his oak bench in a jut of the chimney, with a short pipe in his mouth, and his torn round hat (till he recollected his guest) fixed sideways on his head, like a Dutch peasant; it was an ancient domestic of the old English gentleman, dressed cap-a-pie for the field. A painter, faithful to the apparel of other times, would have noticed the specific articles that formed this kind of character: the short green coat, the black velvet cap, with its appropriate gold band and tassel, the buck-skin gloves and breeches, the belt with its dependent whistle, and the all-commanding whip. Let your fancy assist you in placing these upon the person above described, and the exterior of John Grounds will figure before you. But this will be doing the good old man but half justice. Oh! the heart, the heart; what is the painting of the man, without the portrait of the heart?

Represent, I pray you, to your mind's eye, this venerable personage running into my arms the moment he observed me, exclaiming, in tones which nature never gave the hypocrite—"I beg pardon, sir, for my boldness, but I thought you would like to see me in my old dress, which I have kept ever since in my drawer by itself, and never take it out but now and then of a Sabbath, in summer, and to put an old friend—as your honour, begging your pardon—in mind of old times. I know well enough it don't become me to take such a gentleman by the hand, and hold him so long in my arms, only seeing I have carried you in them from one place to another, all about the premises of the squire's old house and gardens, years upon years———"

After a pause he adverted to the particulars of his dress, assuring me they were the very same things he wore the last year at my father's, except the plush waistcoat, which was a part of my Lady St. John's livery. "To be sure, your honour," said he, gayly, "they are like myself, a little the worse for wear; the old coat, you see (turning it about) has changed colour a bit, from green to yellow; the cap is not altogether what it was; and this fine piece of gold round the crown is pretty much faded; but we are all mortal, your honour knows; but old friends must not be despised."

During this converse, John and Dame Hills may be truly said to have "devoured up his discourse." All he had said had reference to my family or myself—a magnet which had power to draw their attentions and affections at any time. Nor did they neglect the dues of hospitality, which, on my account, and their own, were doubled; and they placed before their guest, with whom they had always lived in good neighbourhood, whatever the farm, its pantry, and its cellar, could afford. "A flow of soul" soon followed this feast of friendship. Grounds had before forgot his fatigue, his long walks, and his new trades; and soon remembered only his fine days of youth, his masters, his kennel, and his former self. "You was too much of a youngling, I suppose," said Grounds, "to recollect the many times I carried you to see my hounds fed, and told you the names of every one of them, and as I gave my signs, bade you bark to Ringwood, and Rockwood, and Finder, and Echo; then put you before me upon Poppet, your father's favourite hunting mare. But I think you can't forget my stealing you out from old Mrs. Margaret, the housekeeper's room, to show you a thing you often wished to see—puss in her form—and your bidding me to take it up gently, that you might carry it home and bring it up tame; then, on my telling you, laughing, it would not let me, your creeping on tip-toe to catch it yourself; upon which it jumped up and set off, and you after it as fast as you could run; and your coming back to me, crying—when it took the headland and got out of sight—' you should have had it, if I, like an old fool, had not made so much noise;' and when I told you you stood a good chance to see it again, and smoking on the squire's table—after giving us a good morning's sport—which, by the bye, was the case, for we had her the very next hunt—you said you did not want to eat, but keep her alive, and make her know you. And when I offered to stick her scut in your hat you threw it at me; and Mrs. Margaret says you would not touch a morsel of it, for spite; ha! ha! ha!"

After some hours, passed in these and in other remarks, which, while they delineate character, and describe the present time and circumstances, renew, and give, as it were, a second life to the past, Grounds took leave of the party with tears, that spoke the sincerity of an apprehension, that he was looking at and embracing me for the last time; and then hurried over the fields, which gave me a sight of him near a mile. And, when his figure became diminished, I did not quit the window, till an interposing hedge shut him wholly from my view.

P. S. The portrait of this laborious, grateful, long-lived, and blessed old man, will be rendered doubly acceptable to the public by the pencil of the elder Barker, as that excellent painter has perpetuated the veteran with his family and cottage, on canvass; whose figures genius will long preserve.

This is a most exquisite performance, and it is to be seen at Mr. Barker's house, Sion Hill, Bath.

REYNARD'S FAREWELL.
By T. Beddoes.

The horses are panting, the bugle has blown,
The hare has passed by, and the partridge has flown:
The hunters are leaving the brow of the hill,
But Reynard alone stands mournfully still;
Deprived of his youth, of his strength, of his pow'r,
These words he repeats in the terrible hour—
" In vain have I hid 'midst the covert of thorn,
To my death I am called by the threatening horn;
In vain have my feet far distanc'd the pack,
Those feet shall he wrench'd and their tendons shall crack;
That brush which was mine since the day of my birth,
Shall be torn from my body, and crush'd in the earth,
Shall be drown'd in the draught which is swallow'd with mirth.
Farewell, ye fair streams, where first I beheld

The form of my bride, where our nuptials were yell'd.
Farewell, thou low cave, where our dwelling we shar'd
Farewell, ye soft herbs, where our couch was prepar'd;
Farewell, thou green farm, which we oft have purloin'd
The straggling fowl, when the banquet we join'd;
Farewell, ye thick woods, where I trembling have laid,
Whilst the bugle has sounded round the broad glade;
Farewell, oh Farewell! I am seiz'd by the hounds;
Farewell, oh Farewell! I die covered with wounds;
Farewell, ye dark woods, each dingle, each dell,
Ye mountains, ye valleys, for ever farewell!"

A SPORTING BIOGRAPHICAL SKETCH OF WILLIAM HABBERFIELD, SLANGLY DENOMINATED "SLENDER BILLY."

Jonathan Wild, in his day, it appears, was not of greater importance to the cross* part of society, than a confidential acquaintance with Slender Billy, rendered essentially necessary towards furthering the exertions of the Family People,† and also to secure them from detection, during the existence of his career. But with this difference—Fielding's Hero possessed all the machinery and baser traits of man: Wild was made up of design—as insensible to feeling and humanity as a rock—and all his calculations were directed to entrap, and then destroy those persons connected with him, in order that he might obtain, without any danger to himself, the possession of their ill-gotten stores. Billy, on the contrary, was not without gene-

* Persons who live by unfair practices.
† Another term for people of the same description, for even slang is not without its synonyms.

rosity of disposition; tenderness to his offspring, and a desire to enrich their minds with learning, a qualification that he was wholly destitute of himself; a heart also that would have done honour to a better cause; and with courage equal to any one; but his notions of honour* in dividing the swag† among his pals, or, in the capacity of an arbitrator, it was asserted, that Sir Samuel Romily never entertained a higher sense of this most noble feeling than did Slender Billy. But, alas! Billy, like heroes of a greater school, could not avert his fate, and very early on the morning of Wednesday, the 29th of January, 1812, he was twisted‡ for his frailties, opposite the debtors' door at Newgate in company with six other criminals. His death excited much public conversation, as he had been known on the town for many years by half the population, particularly in Westminster, from the figure he made in the gymnastic circles, and, also as having been a manager of badger-baitings, dog-fights, &c.

Billy's cabin in the centre of Willow Walk, Tothersfields, was a menagerie for beasts of almost every description, and also a convenient fencing§ repository, from the lady's tyke‖ to the nobleman's wedge.¶ Habberfield, from the

---

* Habberfield's conduct in this respect, was the praise and admiration of all the thieves who had any dealings with him.
†Stolen property. ‡Hanged.
§A receptacle for stolen goods. ‖Lap-dog. ¶Plate.

figure he cut in his menagerical character with the buffer,* or badger-ring was much countenanced by many gentlemen of the fancy,† and particularly by the Westminster collegians, who could have a fund of amusement at all times in the Willow Walks. But Billy's connexion amongst robbers of every description, exceeded by far the patronage bestowed on him by the higher orders in the bull-ring. He always bore the reputation of a man of strict probity in his nefarious dealings, and was considered as the safest fence about town, as his dwelling was suitable to concealment, and garrisoned by buffers, so as to render it impregnable to a sudden attack. Billy was himself a workman too, and accounted as good a cracksman,‡ or peterman,§ as any in the ring, and as close as midnight. He dealt largely in dogs and horses, and several anecdotes are related of his often bargaining for the purchase of each, and on refusal, informing the owners he must have them for nothing, if he could not buy them, and which promise he repeatedly carried into execution. He was a knacker‖ too; and it was a favourite expression of his, that he had stolen many a worn-out horse, rather out of charity to its carcase than the value of its flesh. He had been known for forty years

---

*A bull-dog. †The patrons of bull-baiting, &c.
‡ House-breaker.
§ Cutter away of luggage from carriages, &c.
‖ A killer of horses.

to the police as a cross-cove, technically termed, but had always escaped, until his release of General Austen, and other French prisoners, when he was impeached by his pal, and sentenced to two years' imprisonment. This was the prelude to his misfortune; and such was the generosity of the Frenchman towards Billy, who had thus risked the safety of his person, added to the expenses of procuring a boat and the assistance of other persons to render the escape more certain, that, upon the French General's landing on his native soil, notwithstanding his great promises, Billy was ungratefully bilked of his reward. This piece of ingratitude touched the feelings of Habberfield so keenly, (which often angrily escaped him on the recollection of the circumstance) that he often asserted that he would sooner have forgiven the robbery of his whole menagerie, blunt and all, in one night, than any should have forfeited to him his word and honour, in any transaction that he had been engaged in.

During his imprisonment, being still anxious to turn the penny to account, and blindly flattering himself, from the stanchness of his own conduct towards all his pals who had been previously in trouble, that he was in no danger from conking,* and that " honour" still existed " among thieves," he dabbled a little in forged notes: but

---

* To impose upon any person, under some disguise, &c.

Billy ultimately was sold, and a plant* being put upon him in spite of his caution, led him to his untimely end. The notes were scarcely purchased by the plant, when the office was given to the screws† of Newgate, who were waiting outside of the door of his apartment for the result, when they rushed in and seized violently hold of the person of Slender Billy; but his promptitude of action did not desert him in the hour of distress. Habberfield was a strong man, full of resolution, and determined not to lose a chance while he had any strength left: he wrestled successfully with his keepers, and displayed game‡ that astonished them, by thrusting his hand which contained the marked notes of the plant, into the fire, till they were all burnt, exclaiming, "now it's all right, you may search and be d——d." But unfortunately for Billy, some forged notes were concealed in his bedstead, which he had forgotten, and added to a corroboration of circumstances, he was tried on two counts, one for forging the notes in question, and the other for uttering, knowing them to be forged, and sentenced to death. The Bank, it seems, had been making, some months, great exertions to find out this source; and however singular it may appear, it is an incontrovertible fact, that Slender Billy could not read, although he was

---

*A person sent for the purpose of detecting any one.
†The turnkeys. ‡Courage and manliness.

indicted for forgery! He had a vast number of good notes about him when searched; and it is said, the way he distinguished a large note from the "one pound" was from the length of the words "one hundred," &c.

Upon being double-slanged* after his condemnation, and turned into his cell, his feelings momentarily gave way, and his bursting heart was relieved by a copious shower from his watery ogles.† The shock was now past; his fortitude returned; and he soon resumed his wonted cheerfulness. He divided his property in the most equitable manner between his family; and prepared himself to act upon his notice to quit,‡ with all the regularity of tenant and landlord. He was, as before observed, counted a man of strict punctuality and integrity in his honest dealings; and had saved, it was thought, a large sum of money. His life was offered to him, if he would split§ against the persons who furnished him with the bad notes; but nothing could tempt him from his purpose; urging, that he preferred death to dishonour. That he had also solemnly pledged himself, in common with the rest of his pals, never to impeach the concern under any trouble, and that he was now too game to shrink from his word.

"Besides," he added, "if he did split, he

* Ironed.   †Eyes.   ‡ To prepare for death
§ To impeach any of the gang, &c.

must hang several others, and render their families miserable: and therefore what happiness could he experience upon gaining his liberty, under such reflections, and more especially, to be pointed at as a conk as he walked along, and his life always be in danger. He had no terrors about dying; his mind was made up; and it was in vain to chaff* to him any more on a subject upon which he was immovable." It is confidently asserted, that a pardon was not only offered to be procured for him on the night previous to his suffering, but on the morning of his execution. But he was too game to endanger the existence of his pals: declaring, he should have detested himself in the character of a nose; that he must also have ruined the peace of several other families; have broken his oath; crawled about in secrecy, and his life always have been in danger; he therefore, in the language of his party, mounted the stifler† as cool as a cucumber, and surrendered himself to be twisted without a sigh! Such was the finish of Slender Billy, whose singular exploits, if detailed, would fill a volume.

It was the maxim of Habberfield, that no man required more than six hours rest from his labours, and that the remaining part of the twenty-four ought to be actively employed upon the square;‡ but if that could not be done, a man

---

* To talk.   † The gallows.   ‡ To act honestly.

ought not to remain mousy.* It is pretty generally suspected amongst his confidential friends, that he was the fence, after the ingenious removal, a few years since, of the plate from the Cathedral of St. Paul's. He was likewise suspected of being an extensive gin-spinner,† without the knowledge of the Board of Excise.—It was Billy's boast, that he had not for many years worn a single article of dress that had not been prigged.‡ He left a widow and two daughters.

After his condemnation the following lines were written by a theatrical amateur, who had attended his bull, badger, and dog fetes—

> Ah, wretched Billy! *slender* is thy hope;
>   How could'st thou be so silly?
> *Flash screens* § to *ring* ¶ for home-spun rope.
>   Oh, hapless slender BILLY!
>
> To *badger*,** *bears*,†† and lawyers sage
>   No *Kiddy*‡‡ could be better;
> He'd bear their baiting for an age
>   But now he's *flash'd* §§ the fetter.
>
> His race is run, his days are few,
>   To the ending post he's beacon'd;
> The Jude could *place no more than two*,
>   Poor Billy he was second.¶¶

*Idle.   †A distiller, or keeping a private still.   ‡Stolen.
§Bad notes.   ¶Change.   **Bully.   ††Magistrates.
‡‡Up to a thing or two.   §§Wears.   ¶¶Habberfield was the second criminal tied up at the gallows.

END OF VOL. I.

CONTENTS

OF THE FIRST VOLUME.

A
	Page
ACCOUNT of Cavanah, a celebrated fives player	41
Anecdote of George Morland and the Duke of Hamilton	37
A dog stung to death by bees	32
Anecdote of Pliny	101
Athletic sports in America	112
An epitaph on a spaniel, much lamented by all the members of the Beef-Steak Club	116
Anecdote of Major Topham and Mrs. Wells	122
Animals, birds and fowls, sporting, races, &c. among the Afghauns	129
An account of the Dutch game of Kolven	153
Account of the Highland sports	157
An enormous boar killed in the forest of Wallincourt by the Duke of Wellington	191
An extraordinary shot	197
An ingenious morality on chess, by Pope Innocent	199
A man attacked by weasles	221
An original invitation sporting card	225
Anecdote of Ryley, author of the "Itinerant," and Emery of Covent Garden Theatre	232
Aerial combat	252
A sporting biographical sketch of William Habberfield slangly denominated "Slender Billy," who was indicted for forgery, although he could not read, and executed at the Old Bailey for that crime; his high notions of honour, &c.	267
Anecdotes of the late Lord Orford	226

CONTENTS.

B
	Page
Bear-baiting in olden times	109
Broad sword, cudgelling, &c.	160
Badger-hunting	217

C
Captain Barclay; his various pursuits and attachment to agriculture; his fondness for exercise; his numerous pedestrian feats, with a short account of his noble and ancient origin	9
Cupping on the turf	56
Curious account of a tame seal	136
Colonel Thornton, a thorough bred sportsman, distinguished for his fine collection of sporting subjects painted by the first masters: also his fine breed of blood horses, beagles, terriers, hawks, &c. &c.	171
Curious wager, walking against eating	196
Chess new moves	216
Courage of the stag	222
Crossing the breed of dogs to advantage	236
Curious definition of the title of "A Man of the World"	253

D
Dedication to the Sporting World	5
Duke of Wellington and the shepherd	115
Death of Tom Moody	235

E
Expert slingers in Patagonia	73
Epistle from Tom Crib to Big Ben, concerning some foul play in a late transaction	106
Emma Beagle, a most interesting female sporting portrait	141
Epitaph on a great card player	168

F
Female pedestrianism	112
Ferocity of the lynx	138
Falconry among the ancients	243

G
Great match of walking 1000 miles in 1000 hours	22

CONTENTS. 277

	Page
Great sagacity of the Arabian horse	73
Gallantry of an elephant	84
Gouging match in America	115
Gigantic challenge, a Russian anecdote	247

I

| Inscription intended for the tomb of a noted gambler | 72 |

J

| Jealousy and revenge of a cock | 234 |

L

| Learned ass | 83 |
| Ludicrous angling anecdotes | 250 |

M

Major Topham, of the Wold Cottage, in Yorkshire; a life abounding with interest and anecdotes. Great display of literary talents, and a sportsman of the first order	115
My fancy	152
Major Leeson, a character of great notoriety at one period in the Sporting World	161
Market for singing birds, dogs, &c. in Russia	168
Mode of training the Arabian horse	228
Most extraordinary performance accomplished with a barouche	243

N

Nabob and tiger	35
No coursing in America	115
Neither won nor lost—a wager	249

O

On the advantages resulting from a sound knowledge of training, possessed by that class of society termed the Sporting World	89
Origin of " the *World*" newspaper	123
On viewing an old bench in the park at Windsor, after an absence of thirty years, by Major Topham	127
On the usefulness of pugilism	230
On the qualities of the greyhound	235

P

	Page
Pugilism in Italy	67
Portrait of a jockey, from "Grainger's Characters"	114

R

Raising a regiment of soldiers, in a very short period, by Courtenay, the celebrated Union Irish piper	166
Rusian pugilism	190
Red-deer used in a phæton instead of horses, by Lord Oxford	225
Running in a sack	242
Reynard's farewell	263
Singular pedestrian feat performed with a coach wheel	40
Sporting characters: or, a peep at Tattersall's	48
Sagacity of a greyhound and pointer	81
Sporting song	84
————sketches of British gentlemen in 1819, well known and denominated the Ruffians, the Exquisites, and the Useful Men	85
Singular taste of the town. The sale of a newspaper from the correspondence of two boxers, raised in a higher degree than all the contributions of the most ingenious writers	124
Sagacity of the hedge-hog	135
Sketch of a distinguished sportswoman	141
Singular circumstance of a ball found in the heart of a buck	152
Sporting intrepidity displayed by Mrs. Thornton, in her race over the course at York, against Mr. Flint	184
Sagacity of bees	192
Singular occurrence, a bird caught by a fish	193
Spanish bull-baiting	195
Singular cricket-match and races, between eleven men with one leg against the same number with one arm, all of the men Greenwich pensioners	196
Sporting in the United States, from "A Year's residence &c. by W. Cobbett"	211
Sporting adventure of King Jamie	245

T

The mocking-bird of America	26

	Page
The Moorish wrestlers, with some account of their equestrian performances	30
The late Duke of Hamilton, a first rate sportsman, an excellent cricketer, a great admirer of the pugilistic art, and a man of true courage.	37
The bull bait	40
The bumpkin and the stable-keeper	48
Tiger and lion hunting in Hindostan	57
Trotting upon new principles; or, a hint for the knowing ones at Newmarket	66
The uncertainty of winning	72
The Boa constrictor and the goat	77
The pigeon shooter's glee	80
The mental faculties improved by training	89
The owlery at Arundel Castle	108
The lap-dog, by W. Upton	136
The scorpion	137
The clown and the geese	ib.
The chase of life	138
The horse and viper	139
The chamois, from " Alpine sketches"	155
The archer's song	189
The old Shepherd's dog, by Peter Pindar	192
The honey guide	193
The late Right Hon. Mr. Fox, as a sporting character	198
The humble petition of Duce, an old pointer	203
The ivory-billed woodpecker, of North America	205
The chase—a Shandean Fragment	209
To the memory of Snowball a celebrated greyhound the property of Major Topham	228
The laws of the leash, or coursing; as they were commanded, allowed, and subscribed, by Thomas, late Duke of Norfolk, in the reign of Queen Elizabeth	240
The ruling passion	250
The old English huntsman and mole-catcher	254

U

Unprecedented fear in the sporting world, performed by Mr. Hutchinson, of Canterbury: the freedom of the city voted to him on account of it	74

	Page
United efforts of a pedestrian and a horse	128

V

Voracity of the heron	34

W

Weight for inches	35
Wrestling, pulling the stick, tossing the bar of iron, pitching the cabber, &c	160
Wasps, curious account of	194

Y

Yorkshire fighting	201

Printed in the USA
CPSIA information can be obtained
at www.ICGtesting.com
LVHW022358131124
796582LV00003B/32